THE ABANDONED MINE MYSTERY

THE TED WILFORD SERIES

THE ABANDONED MINE MYSTERY

NORVIN PALLAS

WILDSIDE PRESS

To:
Charles, Judy, William, Nancy, and Cindy Lou

CHAPTER 1.

THE DISAPPEARING CHILDREN

AT least it wasn't an anonymous letter. It was signed by someone named Mrs. Allen, and gave an address in East Walton. If the signature was authentic, the writer deserved consideration.

Ted Wilford, having read the letter, handed it back to Christopher Dobson, editor of the semi-weekly Forestdale *Town Crier.* If Mr. Dobson had saved this letter just to show to him, Ted had a pretty good idea what he had in mind.

Mr. Dobson tapped thoughtfully on the desk with his pencil. "What do you know about matters in East Walton, Ted?"

"Only that the coal mine there shut down almost four years ago, following an explosion. Until I read this letter, I had no idea there was any doubt that it was an accident Mrs. Allen seems to think it was deliberately set off."

"Yes, but she doesn't say who she thinks was responsible. With her husband unemployed and the family on relief, she must be bitter. But why did she keep quiet for four years? And even if the explosion closed the mine, what is keeping it closed?"

"Isn't it the popularity of other fuels, plus the need for automation so they could compete with other people's mines?"

Those are the reasons usually given, Ted, but Mrs. Allen hints something more is involved in this case. Naturally I wouldn't expect you to solve an explosion that happened years ago, no doubt thoroughly investigated at the time and probably an accident anyway—" He *was* talking about a trip, just as Ted had hoped. "But there may be a story here just the same. What is keeping the mine closed, is there any hope of getting it open again, and what are people in East Walton doing about it? A story about a community hard hit by the closing of its chief industry might make a good feature, even though it doesn't justify blazing headlines. How soon will you be ready to leave?"

"Right away. I'm just about caught up with everything here, and I think we could make it to East Walton by dark."

"I take it Nelson could go with you?"

Ted grinned. "It's his car, so it's often a case of his going with me or else I don't go. But I expect he'll be glad to go."

"Tell him to take his camera along. A few pictures to go with your story might be useful."

"How long shall I take on it?" asked Ted, rising to leave.

"Whatever time it takes, Ted. You understand your duties here, and you'll know what's going on up there. It'll be up to you to decide between them. One thing more, Ted," said Mr. Dobson, stopping him. "You know we have our own correspondent up there—Phil Royce. It's only a part-time thing with him, but your going into his territory makes a rather touchy situation. Better talk to him first thing, and explain matters. Good luck, Ted."

It didn't take long for Ted to get hold of Nelson, like Ted home from college for the summer. They packed their suitcases hurriedly, left notes for their families, and within half an hour were on the road to East Walton.

"I don't know what I'd do without you," Ted told Nelson as they *pulled* out of Forestdale.

"You'd hire a car in East Walton, and drive around in style."

"I wouldn't dare put anything like that on my expense account," Ted assured him. "So you are good for something, my boy."

"Thanks for nothing," Nelson answered. "And speaking of work, I guess that working in a coal mine would be just about the worst kind of job. I'd rather go into orbit than do it."

"I can't say I'd exactly love it myself, but why so sure?"

"It's hard work, it's dirty, and it's dangerous. But I wouldn't mind that so much as the fact that it's *spooky*. Just think of working the day shift during the winter. You would go to work before dawn and come home after sunset, and never see the sun at all. You might just as well live in the Arctic."

"Where do the spooks come in?" asked Ted with a laugh.

"Well, just imagine those long dark tunnels, and your lamp throwing big shadows on the walls. You're wandering through there all alone, and your light goes out—it's *black*—not like night outside with the stars and maybe the moon, or clouds reflecting a little light. But absolutely black! You can't see anything at all."

"You don't have to go into the mine if you don't want to," Ted remarked.

"Then you *are* planning to go in?" asked Nelson.

"Probably. But it's up to you whether you go along."

"Oh, I'll go with you, Ted. Might as well live dangerously. Though I suppose it's not really very dangerous," he went on. "It would be quite a coincidence if there was a bad accident on the day and at the place where we happened to be investigating another accident. If the mine is closed, I suppose there's even less chance of an accident than normally."

Ted understood Nelson well enough to know that he was stimulated by danger. Though he was often bored with daily routine, he rose to a challenge like a trout to a fly. There was no better person to depend on in an emergency. Not that Ted had any particular apprehension about danger, even though he had teased Nelson a little about it. Bad accidents were extremely rare, and what could happen just visiting a colliery?

"Of course they *did* have that bad explosion there," Nelson mused. "If we had happened to visit there *that* day, things would have been pretty rough. Just how bad was that accident, Ted?"

"Don't ask me! Four years ago I was more interested in the latest baseball scores than I was in a mine explosion—as long as it didn't happen to anyone I knew. I don't believe it was as bad as it could have been, though. The explosion came while the men were changing shifts, so there weren't many workers down there at the moment."

"Wise me up on the mathematics, Ted," said Nelson. "Since they've already had a bad explosion, does that mean they are less likely to have another one, or more likely?"

"I don't see how it could be less likely—unless the explosion made some kind of readjustment we don't know about," Ted explained. "You never use up your probability. If you have just won a sweepstakes, and then buy a new ticket, your chance of winning is just as good as the next fellow's. But something—something unknown—caused that last explosion, and the same cause might still be at work. I'd say there's a better-than-average chance it will happen again."

"Thanks," said Nelson gloomily. "You've brightened my whole day."

Nothing more was said about danger, and they rode in silence until Nelson remarked casually:

"I've got a riddle for you, Ted. Where's West Walton?"

"West of East Walton, I suppose. Where else could it be?"

"Wrong! Take a look at the map."

Ted took the map from the glove compartment, and studied it for a moment. "I don't see it on the map."

"Right. There's no such place. So why do they call it East Walton, if there isn't any Walton, or West Walton?"

"Maybe there is a West Walton, but it's too little to put on the map."

"That's a pretty definitive map, Ted. And you'll notice that East Walton is on the east bank of the river. Therefore, if there were a West Walton, it would have to be on the other side of the river."

"So . . . ?" asked Ted, realizing that Nelson must have studied the map before they started out.

"Well, do you see any roads on the map, just across the river from East Walton?"

"No," Ted acknowledged, "but there might be small roads the map doesn't show."

"If there were any way to get through there, the map would show it. So if there is a West Walton, it must be terribly small."

Nelson leaned over to switch on the radio. His pushbutton tuning was adjusted for the stations around Forestdale, so he didn't use it now.

"See if you can find East Walton for us, Ted," Nelson requested.

"Why? You want to come in on the beam?"

"Do I have to tell you how to do your work? Isn't it a good idea to find out everything you can about the community you're going into? East Walton doesn't have its own newspaper, or a TV station, so the radio is your best bet."

"That's using your noggin, Nel, old boy. No one can tell *me* you don't have it upstairs, no matter what everybody else says."

Ted had no idea where to find the East Walton station, but fiddled with the dial for some time trying to locate it. When they were nearly there, he figured that the loudest station might well be East Walton, and he left it on while he waited for station identification.

"What's on your own program, Ted?" Nelson inquired. "There are so many places you *could* start, I'm interested to see what the boy wonder will choose."

Ted laughed. "I don't have to choose. Mr. Dobson made it perfectly clear to me. The first thing to do after we're settled in is to look up Phil Royce, our correspondent there. I'm invading his territory, and I'm supposed to get on his good side."

"If he thinks you're an invader, there might not be a good side as far as you're concerned," Nelson pointed out. "How do they work that, Ted? You're not exactly stealing the bread out of his mouth, are you?"

"Hardly that. He works on space rates like I did when I was high-school correspondent for the *Town Crier.* And you know that nobody gets rich on space rates. He probably thinks of it as extra change in his pocket, and some weeks he may have doubts that it's worth the trouble. If you turn in a dozen items, and the paper only uses one, you only get paid for the one that's used, and the rest of your work is wasted. After a while you sort of give up and stop trying so hard. You want to be sure a story is really worth it before you even stir yourself to go after it. Mr. Dobson prefers to pay a salary, but of course he can't afford it with correspondents so far away from Forestdale."

"Then you don't expect trouble with Phil?"

"Not about money. To handle a big story he'd have to put in a lot of work, and at space rates he might not feel it's worth it. But he might take it as criticism that he overlooked a good local story, or that he isn't handling the situation properly. I know that's how I might feel."

Station identification on the radio interrupted them, and it was followed by a news résumé. The national news was reported first, but nothing startling had occurred since the last news summary they had heard. Then the announcer took up local items. Suddenly they really began to listen.

"Mrs. John Llewellyn has reported to the police that her two children are missing. They set out early this afternoon searching for their pet mule, Alice, and nothing has been heard of the two children or the animal since then. The little girl, Joyce, is nine years old and blond. Her brother Johnny is seven years old, and a little darker. Both children were wearing blouses, jeans, and sneakers when last seen. They did not have hats or coats. Anyone seeing the children or the mule is requested to call the police or this station."

"Hope they find them," Nelson commented. "It's a good thing it's not cold out. That helps."

Ted partly turned and stared out the rear window. "Beautiful sunset," he observed.

"What about it?"

"Lots of clouds. It's close to dark, and may rain before very long. I hope those kids aren't in real trouble."

He looked around at the wild rolling hills and the empty woods. There were lots of places where the Llewellyn youngsters could have got lost.

They crossed the river and turned northward toward East Walton. Though Ted had never been here before, he realized that they must be getting very close to the coal mine.

"Hey!" he shouted.

"What's up?" Nelson demanded. Then he realized that Ted wanted him to stop, and he pulled over to the side of the road.

"What do you see up there?" asked Ted. "Aren't those two children?"

Nelson stared. "Two people, anyway. It's hard to tell whether they're children or not, from down here. Take it easy, Ted. Those Llewellyn children aren't the only kids in the world."

"No, but they're the ones we're worrying about right now. Look what they're doing. They're gone now."

"Where did they go?"

"I think that's the entrance to the mine. I've read a little about that mine, and it's a regular labyrinth inside. Come on, let's go."

CHAPTER 2.

NIGHT IN A MINE

IT was a long, steep climb over barren clay soil till they reached the entrance of the mine.

"I wonder how those kids made it," Nelson speculated, as he slipped and went down on his hands, but quickly righted himself and struggled onward.

"Probably they didn't come this way. They may have followed the ridge of the hills."

"What about Alice? You think she could have made it? I know mules go down the Grand Canyon, but I don't think that's as slippery as this."

"Well, we didn't see Alice. She may not have come this way at all."

"But the kids did, and that must mean they *thought* she came this way." Apparently Nelson had accepted the fact that they were following the Llewellyn children.

They reached the entrance to the mine, and paused to look around. The entrance had been boarded up at one time, but the boards had rotted or been broken off. They doubted this was the main entrance to the mine, for there were no facilities for unloading coal or checking in workers. That was probably down at a lower level and invisible from where they stood.

A sign read:

DANGER—NO TRESPASSING

"We don't have any choice, do we, Ted?" asked Nelson.

"No, I guess not."

Once inside they took a dozen steps, then paused once more to allow their eyes to adjust to the gloom. The daylight from the entrance stretched ahead down the corridor, appearing ever more feeble. There was no sign of the children, but there was a turn a little way ahead of them. No doubt Joyce and Johnny—if it was they—had made the turn and were now in the darker, deeper portions of the mine.

Nelson switched on his flashlight, and the beam was feeble enough in the dim glow of daylight. But after they had made the turn, the light seemed stronger and they proceeded more confidently. Looking back they could see a patch of light at the turning, and that was all.

Though he kept the beam aimed mostly at the ground, Nelson occasionally flashed it around the walls. They did not seem to be made of coal. Evidently there had been no mining here—this was merely a corridor cut to reach the seams of coal. Their way led gradually downhill. So far, though there was still no sign of the children, they could not have gone wrong, for there were no branches off the corridor.

"Think that roof will hold up?" asked Nelson, turning the light momentarily on the ceiling of the tunnel.

"It's been there a good many decades. I hope it's good for another hour or two. I don't think we're in any trouble about air, either. There seems to be a draft through here. It's possible that this is an air tunnel, built to carry air down to the lower portions of the mine."

"Wouldn't a tunnel like that be vertical?"

"Maybe, unless this is a double-purpose tunnel."

"Then I suppose the bigger the tunnel the more air you get, and the bigger the tunnel the more likely it is to collapse. How do you decide what to do?"

"I guess it's a good idea to know what you're doing."

They made another turn, and now had lost all touch with the daylight. The walls were beginning to take on a darker hue, as though this were nearing the main lode or vein. How far they had come along the corridor they did not try to guess, but estimated that they were some thirty to fifty feet lower than the entrance. The slope was quite steep, possibly too steep for railway cars, and anyway there was no sign of tracks.

The walls grew progressively blacker, and suddenly they had to make a decision. The corridor branched off in two directions. Apparently this was the point where the mining had begun.

"Which way do we go, Ted?"

"I don't know. Do you think those kids could have a light?"

"They must have. How could they have come this far without one?"

"We never saw a flicker, and they couldn't have been very far ahead of us." He hesitated, indecisive. "Let's try calling."

"OK, but maybe they don't *want* to hear." However, as Ted began to call, "Joyce, Johnny," Nelson joined him. It was a weird sound, though. The calls seemed to echo and reverberate, so that it was impossible to tell from which direction the sound came, or even to recognize the voice of the person calling.

Then they waited silently for a minute or two, hoping for an answer, but none came.

"Probably scared them half to death," Nelson muttered, "if they even heard us."

"If they're within quarter of a mile of us, they heard us," said Ted grimly.

"Well, which way?" Nelson said again.

"Don't you think a right-handed person is more likely to turn to the right?"

"How do we know they're right-handed?" Nelson asked practically. "This corridor to the left looks a little larger, as though it's the main corridor and the other one just a branch."

Shrugging, Ted turned to the left, Nelson close beside him. In a short distance they found themselves in a room from which coal had obviously been taken. They had expected that there would be numerous pillars supporting the ceiling, but now they saw that there were none. The walls of the rooms seemed to act as ceiling props.

"I suppose somebody had to figure out how thick to make the walls and how close together they had to be," Ted observed.

"I'm glad I'm not the one who had to do it," Nelson returned. He flashed his light all about the room, perhaps thirty feet long in its greater dimension. There was no sign of the children, although an opening at the far end of the room apparently led on into another room. "Wait, Ted." He laid a restraining hand on his arm, as Ted seemed to take a step in that direction. "Let's not go any farther. It isn't going to help any if we get lost, too. I've already lost my sense of direction, and if we go much farther I won't even know how far up or down we've come."

"Yes, I guess you're right," said Ted, reluctant to give up, but knowing Nelson was right. "There's nothing more we can do except go for help."

"You mean the police?"

"What else?"

"I suppose you're right, Ted. We have to tell the police, just on the chance it is the Llewellyn children. But I'm not so sure any more. It could have been adults. Adults can walk faster, and if they know where they're going, they could have got way ahead of us. I don't see how children could have done that. At least we should have seen their light."

"Don't you suppose adults might have heard us shouting?"

"Maybe not, if they were far enough ahead. Anyway, why should they answer? *They* didn't need help."

"Wouldn't it sound like maybe *we* needed help?"

"Hm—well, I suppose they would have answered, if they heard us, and if they were here for a legitimate purpose. But just suppose they were up to no good. Then they wouldn't have answered, that's sure. After all, what would adults be doing in an abandoned mine?"

"Maybe they'd like to ask us the same question."

They returned to the point where the corridor divided, and Ted shouted again just for luck. Hardly had the reverberations quieted down when a small voice answered, almost at his elbow:

"Here we are."

Nelson turned the light down, and they saw the two children crouching in a little hollow against the wall, just around the turn to the right. They did not seem frightened, though they smiled a little doubtfully.

"Didn't you hear us calling you before?" asked Ted, as the children left the wall and joined them.

"Yes," Joyce answered. Though the girl and boy were about the same size, she made it clear by taking the lead that she was the older of the two. "But we didn't know who you were."

"I thought you were ghosts," Johnny explained. "I mean, at *first* I thought that."

"Mother told us there aren't any ghosts," Joyce went on, "but Johnny thought maybe you were a new kind that Mother didn't know about yet."

"Where's your light?" asked Nelson suddenly.

"We don't have any light," Joyce returned. "It was awfully dark. That's why we thought we'd better answer you."

Ted and Nelson looked incredulously at the small girl and boy. It seemed impossible that they could have come this far in what was obviously almost pitch dark, and yet that was exactly what happened.

"Let's get out of here," Ted decided. They would all feel better when they were out of this darkness. Even Nelson's flashlight didn't seem as bright as it did before, and feeling their way back to the surface, even though there was no possibility of losing their way, was not appealing.

Nelson took Johnny's hand and led the way, while Ted took Joyce's hand and followed a few steps behind.

"Why did you go into the mine, Joyce? You're not allowed to play in here, are you?"

"No, but we were looking for Alice—she's our mule."

"Yes, I heard about Alice over the radio. Did you see Alice go into the mine?"

"No, but we thought she *might* be in there. And then, when we were walking through the tunnel, we thought we heard her, so we kept on going."

"They must have heard *us* coming," Nelson explained, turning his head back to Ted, "but they couldn't tell which direction the sound was coming from. It's tricky down here."

Ted felt that Nelson was probably right. Surely the children, no matter how brave, would not have had the nerve to keep going into the blackness unless they felt that Alice was just in front of them.

"Alice wears a bell around her neck," Johnny told them.

"Only the bell doesn't always ring, if she walks very slowly," Joyce went on.

"What made you think Alice went into the mine?" Ted inquired.

"Because she used to work in the mine before it closed down."

"Did Alice work with your father?"

"No, we don't have a father. He was killed in the mine."

"Oh." Ted was sorry he had asked this question. "Does Alice like to wander off and go back to the mine?"

"She likes to wander everywhere, I guess. Sometimes she goes to the mine, and sometimes she goes other places. But she always comes back when she gets ready, so maybe she'll come back this time. Did you see her anywhere?"

"No, but we weren't really looking for her. We'll keep our eyes open from now on, and if we see her we'll tell you."

As they approached the mouth of the mine, they suddenly realized that they were not going to get away as soon as they thought. The storm had broken while they were down in the pits. Now the sky was nearly black, thunder pealed, and the rain was pouring down.

"What do we do, Ted?" asked Nelson as they stood at the entrance and watched the storm.

"We can't take the children out now, that's for sure."

"I know, but don't you think one of us had better go and notify the police?"

"On that slippery clay in the dark? You'd break your neck."

"Their mother will be frantic."

"It's better to let people worry than it is to give them something to worry about."

"If that's the way you feel about it, then we'd better plan on staying all night. This rain doesn't look like it's going to let up very soon."

The evening was growing more chilly, and Nelson soon removed his sweater and Ted his jacket, which they gave to the children to wear. Then there was nothing more to do except try to get a little sleep while waiting for morning.

The children had no objection. They curled up on the floor of the corridor, where they soon dropped off to sleep. Sleep was more difficult for Ted and Nelson, who found themselves growing colder, and walked about or occasionally did jump-ups to try and keep warm. The children seemed comfortable enough, though, and oblivious to the hard ground.

The rain had settled down to a steady downpour, and there was no use thinking about leaving before daybreak.

"Well, Ted," Nelson observed, "I'd say you've got a good start on your story already." He nodded back toward the children.

"I guess so," Ted agreed, "but where does it go from here? We've got some digging to do when we get out of this mine in the morning."

"I thought you dug *in* a mine," Nelson said, and ducked a jab from Ted.

Then they sat down with their backs against the wall, and dozed off a little.

CHAPTER 3.

THE RETURN OF ALICE

THE storm ended before dawn. Ted was the first to awaken, feeling cramped and still tired. By the time he had moved around a little Nelson was also awake, denying that he had even been asleep.

"Oh, I may have closed my eyes a little," he admitted. Then he got up, grimacing at his stiff muscles.

It seemed a shame to wake the children, but Ted felt they should be on their way as soon as possible. If the search for the children had been called off during the storm, it would be renewed with the return of daylight.

Nelson agreed it was a good idea, especially as there was nothing for breakfast and they had all missed last night's dinner.

So the children were aroused and led down the hillside toward the car. The clay footing was treacherous after the rain, but they were able to pick their way around the worst spots, and reached the car safely.

"Now for home," said Nelson, starting the car, "but which way is home?"

Joyce indicated the road ahead, and Nelson followed it until she told him to turn off. She pointed out their house just ahead of them. They had driven perhaps a mile altogether, but Nelson figured that it was probably more than that over the hills, the way the children had apparently come.

The Llewellyn place wasn't exactly a farm. It had been a farm at one time, but probably proved unprofitable, and had been divided into several portions, while the men turned to mining instead. The house was quite a way from its closest neighbor, and, though old, looked as though an attempt had been made to keep up appearances.

As the car turned in, a woman came to the door. The children jumped from the car and ran to their mother; their first questions were about Alice. Mrs. Llewellyn shook her head.

"No, Alice hasn't come back yet. I thought perhaps she was with you. But I'm sure she'll be coming home today."

Joyce and Johnny accepted this optimistic prediction, and were satisfied for the time being. Then, holding her children's hands, Mrs. Llewellyn came toward the car. Ted and Nelson got out of the car, and Ted made the introductions.

"I'm surely grateful to you two young men," said Mrs. Llewellyn. "I was worried, of course, but perhaps not quite as worried as I might have been. My children are unusually self-reliant for their age, and I felt sure they'd have sense enough to find some shelter when they saw the storm approaching."

"The storm was no problem," Ted returned. "The mine was a good enough shelter from that." On the way home Johnny had tried to make Ted agree to say nothing about the mine to his mother, but Ted had made no such promise.

"The mine?" said Mrs. Llewellyn questioningly, turning to her children. "You know you've been forbidden to go there, but I suppose with the storm it couldn't be helped. You stayed right by the entrance?"

The children hung their heads, and Nelson felt she might as well know the worst. "They were quite a way in, down to the first branch anyway."

"Children!" Mrs. Llewellyn exclaimed in alarm. Obviously, Joyce and Johnny would hear about this later. "Well, I know everyone's hungry. Come on into the house and I'll make pancakes."

Feeling that it would be rude to refuse her offer, her guests followed her inside. After phoning the police to call off the search, Mrs. Llewellyn set to work in the kitchen. Ted and Nelson were invited to wash up and did their best to clean up, knowing they would have to do something more about their clothes later. Then they all sat down to the table and made short work of the huge pile of pancakes. When Joyce and Johnny had swallowed the last bite, they asked to be excused.

"But don't go off the property," Mrs. Llewellyn instructed them, and they promised, then ran outside.

"That mule!" said their mother with a sigh. "That's what they're after, of course. They won't be satisfied until Alice comes back, and I must admit that I miss her, too. We think Alice is unusually intelligent, and of course the children like to ride on her."

"I don't see how she could be very intelligent," Nelson objected, "if she's still anxious to go back to work in the mines after all these years."

"Oh, I don't think that Alice is at all anxious to return to work. It's simply curiosity. She wants to put her nose into everything that's going on. And I admit she has a mule's stubborn streak. There's nothing you could do to make her change her mind about anything. You might prevent her a dozen times from going somewhere, and that would still be the first place she'd head when she got a chance."

"I know some people just like that," said Nelson with a laugh.

"Well, I'm not at all sure that Alice doesn't think she's a human being," Mrs. Llewellyn remarked, "and the children certainly treat her like one."

"Aren't mules just a little old-fashioned, as far as mining operations go?" Ted inquired.

"It's true there are fewer and fewer mules in the mines today, but they were very useful in the past. They're quite sure-footed, and can handle grades that would perhaps be too steep for the ordinary car on wheels. They're good at negotiating turns, too. If electric power is not available in some portions of the mine, you could use a mule, for gas engines are expensive and smelly and sometimes dangerous inside a mine. And they do have some intelligence. A mule doesn't go plowing blindly into a car up ahead, the way an electric car will."

Ted had previously explained to Mrs. Llewellyn that he was a reporter, and now he told her something about what he was trying to do. She said she would be glad to help him.

"I don't want to appear unnecessarily nosy," Ted assured her, "and I promise not to use your name. We're just trying to get a picture of what is going on here."

"I don't mind a bit, Ted. Though I'd prefer not to have any personal publicity, I would put up with even that, if I thought it would help the children. We're getting along all right, for the time being. We get a monthly check from the state workmen's compensation fund. Then we have some government bonds, which I have managed to hang on to, though I've often been sorely tempted to sell them. My husband was well paid, while he worked, and our living expenses here are quite low. It's the children I am thinking of: how can they get a better education, where will they go, what work can they do? I don't see any future for them in East Walton. There's really nothing here any more."

"Your husband was killed in the big explosion?"

"Oh, no. He died a year—almost two years—before that. I believe that Joyce can just about remember him a little, while Johnny doesn't remember him at all. It was just a 'small' accident—he was the only one who was hurt, and I don't think it ever got into the big papers. But even a 'small' accident can be terribly big, when it concerns the person you love."

"Do you blame anyone for your husband's accident?"

"How can you blame anyone? It could have happened to anyone at any time. A little lapse in judgment, or a little mistake in engineering, and then it happens. I know that's how my husband would want me to look at it."

The telephone rang, but it was in another room, and Ted and Nelson couldn't hear the conversation. Soon Mrs. Llewellyn returned to the room smiling.

"They've found the mule. I must tell the children." She went to the door and called, "Joyce, Johnny! Alice is coming home."

The children were overjoyed at the good news.

"Where was she?" asked Joyce eagerly.

"She was across the river. So you see, Joyce, she was never anywhere near the mine at all."

"No, Mother," said Joyce.

"Across the river, imagine that," said Mrs. Llewellyn, turning to the others. "That means she had to go way down to the bridge, and cross it and come up the other side. She could never have made it under ordinary circumstances. Someone would be sure to notice her and stop her. But I suppose that with the storm, traffic was lighter and she was able to slip across the bridge. You know what this means, Joyce. We'll have to keep Alice tied up after this."

"Oh, no, Mother, please don't tie her up. She hates it so much."

"We'll watch her better next time," Johnny cried.

"Well, we'll see. I do hate to tie her," she explained to the others, "because she resents it so. But the children can't be relied on to close the gate."

"We will, from now on," Joyce pledged, and Johnny agreed.

"I suppose we ought to be going, Ted, shouldn't we?" asked Nelson, rising from the table.

"Oh, no, you have to wait to see Alice," Joyce protested.

"How soon will Alice be here?" Ted inquired.

"It shouldn't be more than ten or fifteen minutes. Mr. Stevens is bringing her home in his truck. If she had to walk, it would be a good deal longer than that. She always comes back, but in her own good time."

Ted remembered the night's fierce storm. "I wonder what Alice did in the rain? Or wouldn't she have minded it?"

"Oh, I don't think Alice would *like* a storm. But she wouldn't let a little thing like that interfere with whatever it was she wanted to do."

"Across the river," Nelson mused. "Would that be in West Walton?"

Mrs. Llewellyn laughed. "That's a local joke. You see, West Walton is one of those places that never really existed. It was planned, and even laid out, at the same time as East Walton. I suppose that under ordinary circumstances East Walton would have expanded a little, and crossed the river. But it never did. For some reason the bridge was never built at East Walton at all. There's one miles below, which you undoubtedly crossed, and then there's a railroad bridge several miles upstream. I don't know whether it was an engineering, economic, or political difficulty, but East Walton never got its bridge. So that was the end of West Walton as well."

"Then West Walton was just a dream?"

"I suppose you'd call it a dream, Nelson, but there are still people who have big plans for West Walton. A promoter has a development all laid out."

They were all outside when the red truck drove into the yard. Mr. Stevens got out, and led Alice, with her bell tinkling, down the ramp from the truck.

Then Mr. Stevens was introduced. He was a red-faced, good-natured farmer from across the river.

"I knew it was your mule, Mrs. Llewellyn, even if I hadn't happened to hear that radio broadcast. I was out looking for her first thing this morning—not really looking for *her,* you understand, but thinking it might help find the children. There aren't many mules left around here any more."

"Has Alice ever been there before?" asked Ted.

"I thought I saw her once last year, and I suppose it was on her mind that the grass was greener over there and she intended to come back. Only the traffic would be too heavy for her, most times."

"How about the railroad bridge?"

"That would be shorter, but I don't think she could get on the right of way. It's fenced off. I sure *hope* she didn't come that way. It would be too dangerous."

He drove off, after accepting the children's thanks for returning their mule. Then Ted and Nelson felt it was time to leave as well. The children tried to persuade them to take a ride on the mule, but they declined, not being quite sure of Alice's friendship at that point.

Finding they could not hold the visitors there any longer, the children made them promise to come back before leaving East Walton, and they drove off amid many shouts of thanks.

"So that was Alice," Nelson muttered. "I thought all mules were named Maude."

"How many mules have you ever known?"

"None, I guess. Half horse and half donkey, with ears that remind you of a rabbit besides—I wonder if Alice really knows what she is?"

"Mrs. Llewellyn seemed to think Alice considers herself human."

"Maybe she does, maybe she does. But I still don't think she'd win any beauty prize."

Ted nodded. "Yes, I'm afraid Alice couldn't win a beauty prize—even in a contest for mules."

CHAPTER 4.

THE BAD SAMARITANS

EXPECTING to arrive in East Walton within a few minutes, the boys were again delayed. They were hardly back on the main road when they passed a car beside the highway, the driver bent over the engine.

"Want to stop and help him?" Nelson inquired.

Ted shrugged. "That's up to you. Maybe he's getting along all right without us."

"No, I don't think so. From the look on his face he seems pretty frustrated. Anyway, the idea is to get acquainted with as many people in East Walton as we can, isn't it?"

He backed up the car and they got out.

"Bad trouble?" asked Nelson.

"Bad enough. Little or big, I can't find it, so it doesn't much matter what it is. I'm stuck here," he answered shortly.

"Let me have a look," Nelson said.

"I hope I didn't sound too ungracious," said the motorist to Ted, as Nelson began to check the engine. "I don't know anything about cars. I've been here an hour already, and looking at that motor is about the same thing as looking at a map of the moon, as far as I'm concerned. If I'd been smart, I would have started hoofing it right away."

"Are you in a hurry?"

"No, except that anything I've got to do would be more important than standing around here, hoping someone will stop to help me. I should have known better. Apparently people around here have never heard about the Good Samaritan."

"You can hardly blame them," Ted pointed out. "You read so much about crime in the newspapers."

"Well, I'm not a criminal. Yes, I am, too. Everybody's a criminal. How could you possibly obey every law that's passed today? Anyway, I'm Patrick Sorrel."

"I'm Ted Wilford, and my friend is Nelson Morgan."

Ted shook hands with Mr. Sorrel, and Nelson nodded.

"I'm grateful to both of you," Mr. Sorrel went on, "though I can't help but be a little sour when I have to depend on strangers for help, while half a dozen people I've known for years drove by without so much as looking at me."

"Friends of yours went by without stopping?" asked Ted.

"I didn't say they were friends. I said they were people I knew. I don't have any friends."

Ted was thinking how odd that sounded when Mr. Sorrel went on to explain:

"You might think it's all my fault, and it is possible you are right—but that doesn't necessarily follow, either. People don't like me because I'm ambitious and want to better myself. Does that sound like such a crime?"

"No," Ted agreed cautiously, "but it might depend on how you went about it."

"I'm not stealing the savings of widows and orphans, if that's what you mean. I have a straight-forward business proposition."

"Just what is your business, Mr. Sorrel?"

"I'm a real-estate promoter, or at least I'm trying to be one. I'm developing the property across the river, known as West Walton. That's been a dream around here for generations, and I'm trying to make it come true."

Nelson looked up suddenly from his work. "West Walton? We've been talking about you lately—only we didn't know that you were the person we were talking about."

"Do you own the property of West Walton?" asked Ted.

"I own some of it outright. I control most of the rest of it through leases and options. You may hear stories that I cheated people, paid them less than the property was worth, but don't you believe them. We agreed upon price, and I paid whatever seemed a fair value at that time. Now do you see anything dishonest about what I'm doing?"

"Sounds all right, the way you describe it," Ted agreed. "Just why do people have it in for you?"

"I'll tell you why," said Mr. Sorrel bitterly. "It's because I wasn't satisfied to be a coal miner. The miners seem to think I've deserted them. How is it going to hurt East Walton if I build a nice section of homes in West Walton? They will be for wealthy retired people, and the executive and professional type of working people. I'm afraid they'd be outside the reach of most coal miners—even if the mine were open."

Ted smiled a little ruefully. "Haven't you answered your own question? People resent you because you *are* catering to a wealthier class of people, and more or less leaving them stranded."

"Well, what do you expect me to do?" said Mr. Sorrel sharply. "Coal mining is a dead issue, as far as East Walton is concerned. We were all caught in the same trap. I've managed to wriggle out— maybe—by the skin of my teeth. It's up to the others to try to figure out some way of wriggling out, too. If they sit around waiting for the mine to open again, I think they're in for a long, long wait."

"Is it really that bad?" Ted questioned.

"I'm afraid it is, Ted. Everything is booming except coal, and that's fallen way, way off. You might almost as well raise your son to be a blacksmith as a coal miner."

He was painting a pretty dismal picture. But was that all there was to the story?

"What do the people in East Walton think about it?" asked Ted.

"That's just it, they don't think. The people who think have left already, and the children are all planning to leave, just as soon as they are old enough. All the others have settled down into a poverty-stricken apathy. How are you making out, Nelson?"

Nelson beckoned to him. "See that nut down there?"

"Don't try to explain it to me. I don't know the first thing about engines. The important thing is, can you fix it?"

Nelson shook his head. "I think you need a new part." He wiped his hands on a rag.

"Well, then," said Mr. Sorrel, in exasperation, "how about giving me a lift into town where I can hire a mechanic? I'd better lock up my car, in case some juveniles are prowling around."

"What do you make of this guy, Ted?" Nelson asked in a low voice. "Isn't he a screwball?"

"Maybe he just acts that way."

"Act that way long enough, and he's likely to *be* that way," Nelson muttered, but had no time to say more as Mr. Sorrel returned to them.

They piled into the front seat of Nelson's car and had barely started when Mr. Sorrel said:

"If you're not in a hurry, you might turn off on this little side road. It'll take you closer to the river, and you'll be able to see my development."

So they turned off onto a dirt road that cut between two hills, then circled around behind them along the river bank. Chances were that this road might be under water in flood time, and that was the reason it had not been developed.

"Draw up here, Nelson," Mr. Sorrel suggested. "Now, you see that?" Mr. Sorrel pointed with pride. "That's West Walton."

"Hm, the grass *does* look greener on the other side," Nelson murmured.

"What's that?"

"Just a private joke."

Ted regarded the green, gentle hills. "Is there anything over there?"

"Surveyors' stakes, and things of that sort. It's all laid out. All that's necessary is for my bank loans to come through, and we'll be ready to shovel dirt."

"Expecting any trouble there?"

"There's always the possibility of trouble, but I'm not expecting any. I expect to finance it one way or another."

He turned to Nelson. "How do you like the view?"

"Pretty nice, but I don't think I'd like to retire by a river. That flowing water always reminds me that I ought to be up and doing things."

"Aren't we on the wrong side of the river?" asked Ted.

"What do you mean, Ted?" Mr. Sorrel responded.

"It isn't so important what sort of view we have from here. What's important is what sort of view they have from over there."

"There're some pretty hills over here, Ted. There's the coal mining, of course, but that doesn't mean much. Anyway, I don't expect to see it renewed in my lifetime."

Nelson drove on slowly along the curving road, until it had rejoined the main highway. In a few minutes they had reached the outskirts of East Walton. The small city, though close to the river, did not share the view they had just seen, for it was cut off by a low range of hills. Following Mr. Sorrel's directions, they dropped him off at a small auto repair shop.

"I can handle everything from here on. Thanks for the lift, and for listening to my babbling," said Mr. Sorrel, and with a wave of his hand he left them.

"So that's West Walton," Nelson murmured. "You might better call it 'Sorrel's Pastures.' "

"Funny how you can have so much prosperity on one side of a river," Ted said, "and so much poverty on the other."

"It's still a pasture over there," Nelson reminded him. "The coal mine might come back before those homes are ever built. You think he's got any customers yet?"

"I don't suppose so, but I don't think he'll have any trouble selling them—if and when he gets them built. It's a nice quiet little community, but still not too far away from some big cultural centers."

"And if he does get them built, then what is poor little Alice going to do? She won't be able to go across the river to eat some of that nice green grass on those open, rolling hills. Say, Ted, where would a mule go during a storm?"

"Does it matter?"

"I'd just like to know, that's all. I think Alice is too smart to stay out in a storm like that, and anyway she didn't look like she'd been drenched. We know she wasn't in the mine, so where was she?"

"Suppose you tell me."

"I think maybe somebody sheltered her."

"And then what?"

"Took her across the river by truck after the storm was over."

"Why in the world would anybody do that?" Ted asked.

"How should I know? I don't figure things out, I just have fun. Why?" he said, noticing a suddenly startled look on Ted's face. "Did I say something brilliant?"

"I'm not sure whether you did or not. It does seem an awful way for Alice to go all by herself. I don't see how she could have made it except by walking through the rain last night—and I agree she didn't look particularly bedraggled. I should think her normal reaction when the storm came up would be to forget all about that green grass across the river, and turn around and head for home and shelter."

"Are you forgetting a mule's one-track mind, Ted?"

"Maybe I am," admitted Ted.

"Any chance that Alice *swam* across the river?"

Ted frowned. "She didn't look as though she had been wet. And then, both Mr. Stevens and Mrs. Llewellyn assumed right from the beginning that Alice must have gone around by the road. Apparently it never even occurred to them that she might have swum."

"Do we have a mystery here, Ted?"

"We didn't, until you started something going—I don't know whether it was your head or your tongue."

"My tongue," said Nelson.

"Well, where does it leave us? We don't know where Alice went, but we don't think she got wet. If she didn't, that eliminates the possibility of swimming the river, or going around by the road during an all-night storm. Somebody could have sheltered her, then taken her across the river early this morning in a truck or delivery wagon, and dumped her off. But why would anyone want to do a crazy thing like that?"

It was Nelson's turn to look suddenly startled. 'Ted," he said, "don't think I've flipped, but look at it this way: what always happens after the mule runs away?"

"Why—the children go out to look for her, I suppose."

"Right. Do you think the idea was to lure the children out?"

Ted shook his head. "That doesn't make much sense, either. They're not wealthy, so why kidnap them? Just the same, you've got me stirred up. I want to find out where Alice spent last night. Maybe there's a simple answer, but let's try anyhow."

CHAPTER 5.

MRS. ALLEN'S ACCUSATION

IT was agreed that any suspicions the boys had about Alice's trips should be kept strictly to themselves.

"We don't know who's who in town yet," Nelson pointed out, "and if we get to talking, it may reach the wrong person."

"Yes, and I'm not anxious to upset Mrs. Llewellyn, either, about something that may be nothing more than a wild idea."

Nelson shook his head. "I'm not so sure it's a wild idea, Ted. A person would only need to lure the children to the mine and let them lose themselves. And maybe that's just what would have happened if we—if you—hadn't seen them in time. No matter how poor they are, they could be heirs, or something like that."

"I just can't believe it, Nel. Nobody could be that mean to children, for the sake of a little property."

"Don't count on it, Ted. Some people are mean enough for anything. If there's even a chance we're right, shouldn't we go to the police?"

"And tell them what? After all, maybe some kind-hearted person noticed Alice this morning, dried her off and combed and brushed her a little, then sent her along her way. It might be as simple as that."

"But let's keep our eyes and ears open just the same," Nelson suggested, and Ted agreed.

They had spotted a motel near the edge of town, and had no trouble engaging a cabin. They cleaned up and took care of their clothes in a self-service laundry. Ted looked at his watch.

"Eleven o'clock. Do you want some lunch, or shall we go looking for Phil Royce?"

"Let's go talk to Royce. I can wait awhile for lunch, after those pancakes. And *after* lunch I'm going to sleep. Last night wasn't the most comfortable one of my life. By the way, what do you know about Phil Royce?" asked Nelson, as they set out in the car.

"Not a whole lot. He's a good correspondent—always sends in more copy than we can use. I don't think there is much going on that escapes him. But he never seems annoyed when we can't use every- thing. His copy is neat, and he always respects our deadlines—every- thing comes in on time."

"You're talking about his copy," Nelson objected. "What about him?"

"I've never met him. I hear he's an intelligent and pleasant per- son. He's young, has had some college. He works in his father's drugstore. That's probably it on the corner up ahead. There might not be more than one in a small place like this."

Ted's guess was right, but the shades on the display windows were down, and there was a sign on the front door that read:

Open again at four p.m.

"Closed at this time of the day?" asked Nelson, puzzled. "How do they expect to get any business?"

"Maybe Phil and his father had to attend to personal matters, and there's no other clerk."

"Do you suppose they always pull down their shades when they close up?"

"Maybe they're changing window displays," Ted suggested.

They walked past the store and looked at the side of the building. There seemed to be living quarters on the second floor, in the rear of the building, but there was no sign that anyone was at home just then. The boys returned to the car having agreed to return at four.

Consulting their watches, they decided there might be time to call on Mrs. Allen before lunch, "If there is a Mrs. Allen," said Nel- son skeptically. "If she's a busybody, she probably wouldn't sign her right name to a letter."

"She sounded more worried than malicious," Ted recollected.

They stopped at an outdoor telephone booth, and Ted found Mrs. Allen's name in the directory. He put through a call, and it turned out that this was the right Mrs. Allen. She acknowledged writing the let- ter, but she answered cautiously.

"I didn't think anyone would come all the way to East Walton about the letter, Mr. Wilford. I was really hoping that Mr. Dobson would print an editorial about it."

"As long as I'm here, is it all right if I stop in to talk with you?"

"Well . . . when do you want to come?"

"I can come right now."

"Come along now, then."

"Thank you, Mrs. Allen. Goodbye," but he hung up with a feeling that Mrs. Allen's invitation was most reluctant. "I wonder why she wasn't happy about it?" he asked of Nelson. "You'd think she'd be glad that she managed to stir up a little action."

"Maybe that's the whole trouble, Ted. She may be afraid of just what she did stir up."

But as soon as they arrived at the Allen home, and were admitted to the living room, they realized what the trouble was. Mr. Allen was there, too, and he told them that he had not known about his wife's letter until Ted called. Obviously, the Allens were arguing about it.

"I still say you shouldn't have written to the newspaper, Mary," said Mr. Allen, after all the introductions had been performed. "You don't have a shred of proof. If Mr. Dobson had printed your letter, you could have been sued for libel."

"I asked him not to print it," she replied, "but suppose someone did sue us, what difference would it make? We have nothing they could take from us."

"I'm sure Mr. Dobson wouldn't have printed such a letter without proof," said Ted, "but we would like to know more about the situation."

"You've wasted your time coming here," said Mr. Allen bluntly. "We can't tell you anything that you will be able to use. After all, there was a safety inspection following the explosion."

Nelson spoke up for the first time. "What was the conclusion?"

"That the miners, in setting off an explosion, had happened to touch upon a gas pocket inside the wall, giving them a much bigger explosion than they had bargained for. It's just one of those things that happens once in a million times. There's no way you can guard against it, except to be as careful and alert as you can at all times."

"How could the committee know what caused the explosion," asked Mrs. Allen scornfully, "after all the evidence was blown up?

I'm sick and tired of the way everyone has whitewashed that terrible man. Mr. Sorrel prospers while the rest of us live on charity and wonder how we're going to educate our children."

Mr. Sorrel! Ted and Nelson looked at each other, and Mr. Allen noticed that they did so.

"Do you know Mr. Sorrel?"

"We've met him," said Ted.

Mr. Allen turned to his wife. "Now do you see what you've done? You've made a vicious charge against a responsible man—in front of witnesses. If that should get back to Mr. Sorrel, he would have a sound basis for a slander suit."

"Then let him sue," said Mrs. Allen bitterly. "He would have to sue the whole town. I'm only saying what everyone else is saying, too—though not openly, of course."

"I can promise you that what you say here won't go any further," said Ted with a frown. "But I would like to know just what basis you have for your charge against this man. If the safety committee declared it to be accidental, I don't see how anyone else can claim it was not."

Mrs. Allen looked at her husband, who shrugged his shoulders as though to say that the damage had already been done. With this encouragement to go on, Mrs. Allen continued:

"I don't think the report of the safety committee means anything at all. The committee doesn't know what caused the explosion, and so they are making the best guess they can. And remember, all the evidence didn't come out at the hearings. There was evidence that no one had the courage to step up and present to them."

"What evidence?" asked Ted sharply.

"There was the timing of the explosion, for one thing. Now I'm sure, in spite of my low opinion of him, that Mr. Sorrel never really intended to kill anyone. The explosion went off between shifts—or when the shifts would normally have been changed. There was an exception that day for some reason. Many of the workers were out, but some remained in the mine. The miners, or a supervisor, knew about the change, but Mr. Sorrel didn't. It had to be somebody who knew something about what was going on, but not everything."

"Then Mr. Sorrel wasn't a miner at the time?"

"No, he was the head of the union. You see how that fits in? He did know about the different shifts, but not about the change that had been made."

"And so did a lot of other people," Mr. Allen objected.

She turned to her husband. "Then what about that visit he made to the state safety committee, just a few days, or a week, before the explosion?"

"Wouldn't that tend to clear him?" Ted inquired. "His concern with safety must have been because he suspected something was wrong. Did he ever explain why he went to the committee?"

"Yes, he said he wanted some information about gas and gas explosions. I think it was just a cover-up, so he would have something to blame the explosion on."

Though Ted didn't think much of this point, Mr. Allen backed his wife up. "There was something a little strange about that visit to the committee, Ted. It's never been explained just what he suspected. If he really thought a dangerous situation existed in the mine, as union steward he should have demanded that the mine be closed until it could be corrected."

"And then," Mrs. Allen went on eagerly, "he resigned from the union right after the explosion. He wasn't interested in the men, or their problems, or getting the mine back open again. He was determined to get the mine closed, and now that he had had his way, there wasn't anything more for him to do."

"Well, I don't know about that," said Mr. Allen, more cautiously. "He may have felt that there was little chance of getting the mine open again, and that he had better get into something more profitable." The miner spread out his hands to examine their backs. "My hands are finally clean again, after all these years, though I must say that I'd much prefer to have them dirty, if it would mean getting back to work. That grime eats into your knuckles so that you never have clean hands, no matter how often you wash them. In a way there's something respectable about dirt, especially in a coal-mining town, where people are likely to be suspicious of a man whose hands are always clean. That's how a good many people feel about Mr. Sorrel. They think he didn't want to have dirty hands, like all the rest of us."

"I'm afraid I don't understand," said Ted. "Just why would Mr. Sorrel want the mine closed? How could that be profitable to him?"

Mr. Allen looked surprised. "Didn't you hear about his housing development, across the river in what he calls West Walton? Do you think retired millionaires want to look across the river at a busy coal mine?"

"We were out there this morning," Nelson pointed out, "and it didn't look so bad to us."

"Maybe not, but before the explosion there was talk of strip mining. You know how strip mining pretty generally tears up the landscape. You work from the surface, and go down with bulldozers and get the coal with no nonsense, and you get it all. No tunnels, or anything like that. State law requires the mining companies to do something to restore the landscape when they are finished. But the mining might go on for many years, and afterward the attempt to restore things might be pretty ineffective."

"Was strip mining being considered for the East Walton mine?" Ted asked.

"It was under consideration for at least part of the mine."

"I should think the explosion in the mine would make the possibility of strip mining more rather than less likely," Nelson observed.

"Well, I'm only telling you what people think. If he could cripple the mine badly enough to make it close, it might be difficult to open it again. Everybody loses money with the mine closed, and the financial position of the company would get steadily worse."

"I'd been wondering about that," Ted remarked thoughtfully. "After the explosion, and a safety inspection, why wasn't the mine reopened? Even if this man caused the explosion, he couldn't have kept the mine closed."

"The way things are going with the coal industry, Ted, it was pretty much touch and go. A good deal of equipment had been destroyed, and the explosion suggested the need for further changes. And the money just wasn't there."

"I don't know that the newspaper will be able to do much about the explosion, Mr. Allen, but I'm pretty sure that Mr. Dobson intends to run a story about East Walton. Would you mind telling me how the closing of the mine has affected you? Have you ever considered leaving East Walton?"

"How could I leave here? I've been a miner for thirty years. How could I learn a new trade at this stage of my life? Of course I'd rather be working, but it seems my best chance is to sit tight and wait for the mine to open."

He told them that he had two children of high-school age. He was determined they would get their diplomas, and then he was going to send them away with his blessing.

He talked about some of the other unemployed miners. "I can tell you how it is. People can't afford the big things in life, so they settle for the little things instead. Education is one of the first things that is abandoned. Then insurance, so that any sort of emergency becomes a catastrophe. Home ownership goes, people make do with old appliances, health is neglected."

Finally Mr. Allen gave Ted the names of a dozen people to interview, including the president of the mine, the present head of the union, the mayor, and others. Then, thanking both the Allens, the boys took their leave.

CHAPTER 6.

FELONIOUS ENTRY

THINK they've really got anything on Mr. Sorrel, Ted?" asked Nelson as they got into the car.

"Nothing that would hold up in court, that's certain. I'm really surprised that they could suspect him of such a thing. I don't suppose everybody does, but apparently a great many people do. It seemed strange when he told us about no one offering to help him on the road, but I can understand it now."

"Are you going to talk with Mr. Sorrel again?"

"Sure, I'm more anxious to talk to him now than before."

"Are you going to accuse him of setting off the explosion, or just ask him if he did it?"

"I'm certainly not going to accuse him. Mr. Dobson would have me off the staff in ten seconds flat if he heard about that. And I don't suppose there's much point in asking him, either. But it will be interesting to see what he has to say, now that we know a little more about him."

"He didn't mention the explosion when he talked to you this morning, did he?"

"No, and why should he help spread rumors about himself? But he didn't know I was a reporter, either. He'll know that soon enough, if I go around talking to all the people on this list, and he'll figure I'm nosing into something."

"He's in something of a spot, all right. How could he prove that he *didn't* do it?"

"No way that I know of, except by finding the guilty party."

"And what if there isn't any guilty party, that it was just an accident as the safety board decided?"

"Then I guess he's just out of luck."

They found a neat little snack bar where they had lunch, and then returned to the motel. Both were feeling tired after less than two or three hours' sleep the previous night. But after a nap and a shower they were ready to look up Phil at the drugstore.

"Are we going to tell Phil anything about what the Allens told us?" Nelson asked Ted as they walked the few blocks to the store.

"We promised not to, remember? Anyway, a good reporter doesn't tell everything he knows."

"That's all right by me, Ted, only I thought maybe Phil was like a member of the family."

The sign on the door had been removed, but the shades were still down. Until they tried the door and found it open, they were not sure if the store was ready for business. But inside a scene of confusion greeted them. Packages had been swept off the shelves, magazines were lying about on the floor, and there was even some broken glass here and there. A young man was trying to put things to rights. He looked up inquiringly as they entered.

"I'm Ted Wilford of the *Town Crier,*" said Ted, extending his hand.

"Oh, Ted, how are you?" Phil exclaimed, coming out from behind the counter to greet him. "Glad to see you. I've certainly heard a lot about you."

"And I've read enough of your copy to feel that we're acquainted," Ted responded. "This is Nelson Morgan, who takes pictures for us once in a while," and Nelson and Phil also shook hands.

"What goes on here?" asked Nelson, sweeping his arm about in a wide arc.

"Burglary," said Phil disgustedly.

"Lose very much?" asked Ted.

"Not really. Thirty or forty dollars in cash, and they picked our merchandise over, apparently knocking down everything they didn't want to take. It was a bunch of juveniles, I suppose. Professional burglars only take what they want, and don't ask for trouble."

"Were you at home at the time?"

"Yes, but I was the only one home, and I sleep like a log. Anyway, my bedroom is in the rear, and sound doesn't carry very well."

"Still, it must have been someone who knew his way around pretty well."

"I suppose so. And another thing he would have to know is that our burglar alarm is just a decoration. It's been out of order for years, and somehow we never felt we could spare the money to get it fixed. Of course we didn't broadcast the news, but I guess these kids have ways of catching on.

"Anyway, you got yourself a story for the *Town Crier,*" Nelson remarked.

"No, I don't think so, Nelson," Phil answered. "I hate to say it, but things like this are sort of commonplace around town ever since the mine closed down."

"It sounds like a tough situation," Ted acknowledged. "By the way, we stopped in earlier, but the store was closed."

"Yes, I had to go down to the police station for a while, and then I wanted the insurance adjuster to see everything the way it was, before I started cleaning up. He was here a little while ago. We're close to an agreement, but he wants as accurate a list as I can make up of what was taken."

"Don't you have some narcotics and other dangerous drugs?" asked Ted.

"Yes, but we keep them in a separate locked compartment. Nothing was touched there, which makes it seem more than ever like the work of juveniles."

Then Phil asked them about their errand.

"Something came up that made us think about East Walton and the closed mine, and Mr. Dobson suggested that I run up here and look the situation over. So I rounded up my photographer and chauffeur, and came along. I hope there won't be any misunderstanding about this story, Phil. It isn't that Mr. Dobson didn't think you could handle it, but it was outside the regular routine. Of course, if you're interested, I don't see why we couldn't work on it together."

"That's generous of you, Ted, but no thanks." Phil waved his hand at the debris about him. "It looks like I'm going to have my hands full here for a while. Even under normal conditions I'm more or less tied up here at the drugstore. My father and I are trying to run it between us—we can't afford to hire any additional help—and that keeps me pretty busy. Anyway, I think you're a better man for this particular job than I am. I'm going to have to go right on living here, even after the story appears. That means I'd have to be a little cau-

THE ABANDONED MINE MYSTERY | 39

tious about whose toes I stepped on. If you come up with a story that might do East Walton any good—and I know that's what you have in mind—then you'll have to come in here, get your own facts, form your own judgments, and let the chips fall where they may. It would take an outsider to do that."

"I'm glad you see it that way," said Ted, much relieved. "I appreciate it."

"That doesn't mean I'm not interested in this story, Ted. After all, we both work for the same paper. If there's anything I can tell you, or anybody I can steer you to, just let me know. By the way, whom have you talked to already?"

"Not very many people. There's Mrs. Llewellyn—we happened to run into her children when they were out looking for their mule." Phil did not seem at all interested in the mule, but looked up as Ted went on: "And then we came across Mr. Sorrel stranded on the road this morning, and had quite a long talk with him."

"Patrick Sorrel—there's a man for you. He's not really a clown; he's got a good deal more on the ball than he shows at first. But let's see if I can guess what he told you. First he said everybody in town hated him, right?"

"That was one of the first things," Ted admitted. "But he seemed to have something to back him up. He said half a dozen people he knew passed him up while he was stranded on the road."

"Probably true," said Phil. "Would you stop to help a man who might snap your head off? When a person says everybody in town hates him, what he probably means is that he does the hating."

"Why should he hate everybody?" Nelson inquired. "Does he have any reason?"

"He doesn't hate people as people, but what they stand for. It's the coal mine, and the dirt, and the danger, and the poverty, and the ignorance that burns him. The miners felt that as a union official he should have been in there fighting to get the mine open again. Instead he walked out. Then it came out that he had been working on this property development scheme of his for years, even while he was acting as a union official. Naturally, the miners feel that while he was representing them, or 'pretending' to represent them, as they call it, he was really more interested in his own scheme. And when they see those fine homes going up across the river, and compare it with their own poverty—well, people are only human."

"Won't a development like that brings jobs to the community?" asked Nelson.

"Oh, yes—surveyors and contractors and masons and carpenters and electricians and all the rest. But not coal miners. Workers in East Walton are going to feel left out once more."

"I can see where people in East Walton might feel that Mr. Sorrel had deserted them," said Ted, "but still it seems kind of petty to leave him stranded out on the road."

"You've encountered that famous personality of his, haven't you, Ted? For some reason he can't talk to a person for five minutes without insulting him—and it doesn't matter who it is."

Apparently Phil wasn't going to mention the explosion, so neither did Ted or Nelson.

"How have things been going with you, Phil?" Ted asked then.

"Oh, the closing of the mine hurt us almost as much as anyone. Our business took a nose dive, and has never really recovered since. I was a high-school correspondent for our local paper, the way you were, Ted, when the explosion came. It was a big enough story so that I covered it along with the rest of the staff. It was my last important story. I went off to college to study pharmacy, but my money ran out in the second year, and I came home. Our local newspaper had died by that time, but I latched on to the *Town Crier* as a correspondent. It's not as good as having our own local paper, of course, but Mr. Dobson tries to be fair."

"Would the opening of the mine help you get back to college?" asked Nelson.

"It sure wouldn't hurt anything. But I don't know—I'm not sure that this mine is ever going to open again. And if it does automation may eliminate a lot of jobs anyway."

But if he wasn't figuring on the mine getting him back to college, Ted wondered, what would he do?

"If you want to talk to some young people, Ted, why don't you stop in at the Teen-agers' Canteen tonight? I won't be able to stay the whole evening, but I'll be able to introduce you around a little."

Both Ted and Nelson thought this was a good idea, and agreed to meet him there. Then they took their leave.

That night Phil introduced the boys to a number of students and ex-students. There was a juke box going, and Ted was soon dancing with a high-school girl named Estelle. Although he was not advertising the fact that he was a reporter, Estelle remembered his by-line on some stories in the *Town Crier.*

"Are you going to stay on in East Walton, Estelle?" he inquired.

"Oh, no. Hardly anyone is—just a few who have no ambition, or are too tied down with responsibilities here, or have hopes of other kinds of jobs besides coal mining. None of us kids has much confidence in the mine any more."

"What are your plans, Estelle?"

"I'm better off than most. My father is an unemployed coal miner, too, but I have an aunt who is going to help me through college. I plan to become a music teacher. I'm only waiting to get my high-school diploma. Most of the high-school graduates can't go on to college, unless their fathers happen to be prosperous coal pirates."

"Coal pirates? What are those?"

"Haven't you heard about the coal pirates? Well, you know the mine is closed, but there are really a good many miners working down there. They come and go as they please, and dig coal for their own profit."

"Doesn't the company try to stop them?"

"Mr. Winslow, the president, is pretty tolerant about it. He figures they can't get away with much, and if it helps some of the most desperate cases, then he's willing to overlook it."

"Do the pirates manage to earn very much?"

"I don't suppose they do, although there's a lot of joking about it under cover. No one talks about it, although everyone knows that it's going on."

"Is your father one of the coal pirates?"

"Oh, no. Some people think it's all right, and some don't. My father doesn't."

None of the talk changed Ted's viewpoint about East Walton. Young people felt there was nothing for them in this community. Even if the mine opened again, they would be left out. Their only reaction was to get out of town as soon as possible.

Ted and Nelson decided to leave the Canteen early, and drove back to the motel quickly, only to find an officer awaiting them.

"Are you Nelson Morgan?" he asked, sticking his head in the window on the driver's side, and Nelson nodded. "I've been waiting for you. Mind if I search you, young man?"

CHAPTER 7.

BIG TROUBLE

THE boys stared at the patrolman. What could he be after, and what were their rights in the matter? Surely an officer had no right to search a person unless he had been behaving in a suspicious manner. Where did that leave them?

"Do we have to allow it?" asked Ted, who seemed to be included in the officer's invitation.

"No, you don't."

Ted and Nelson looked at each other. They couldn't see how a search was going to hurt them any, and it might help to speed up matters. Nelson gave a little shrug to say that it was up to Ted, and he said:

"OK, go ahead."

The patrolman went ahead with the job, apparently without finding what he was after.

"Any objection if I search your car?"

Nelson looked at Ted once more. "I guess not."

Having already locked his car, Nelson got out the key and handed it to the officer. He opened the door and patted around the seat cushions. Next he looked in the glove compartment, then reached in his pocket for a handkerchief and used it to lift something out. The boys were stunned to see that it was a revolver. A gun in their car?

"Is this yours?" asked the officer.

"No," Nelson said angrily. "I never saw it before."

"Neither did I," Ted added, as the officer turned toward him.

"Actually, carrying a gun in your car isn't such a serious offense," the officer went on. "If it is your gun, I advise you to admit it, since we can probably check on it anyway."

"Why admit something that isn't so?" Nelson demanded.

"In that case, I think you'd better come along to the station until we see if the gun can be identified."

"Are we under arrest?" asked Ted.

"No. Since you seem to be under twenty-one, I'll give you a word of unofficial advice. If you've got anything to hide, don't say anything until you've consulted a lawyer. But if you haven't, then the more cooperation you give us, the sooner we can probably get this thing cleared up. Which way do you want it?"

"We'll cooperate," Nelson decided. "Shall I drive in my car?" and the officer nodded.

The boys got into their car and drove off, with the patrol car close behind.

"How about this, Ted? The officer knew who I was before we got there, and he knew what he was looking for, too. As soon as he found the gun he stopped looking for anything else. That means he must have had a tip the gun was there."

"Yes, and who could have tipped him off, except the person who put it there?"

"Won't the police know who gave them the tip?"

"Probably not. Most likely it was an anonymous telephone call. Remember how careful he was to ask our permission about everything. They wouldn't need our permission if they had a warrant, and even a signed complaint might give them more authority."

"Well, then, what *else* did this anonymous caller tell them? We may be in more trouble than just having a gun in our possession."

At the station they parked the car, and the officer followed them inside. "Here they are," he announced to the desk sergeant. "I found this revolver in the glove compartment of their car."

"You know what to do with it." The officer nodded, and left the room. "What are your names and addresses?" the sergeant asked, without looking at them, and they told him. "Do you have any identification?"

Both had driver's licenses, which they produced. The sergeant examined them and then Ted handed him his press card.

"Are you here on assignment, Wilford?" he inquired.

"Yes, I am."

"Then you won't mind if I verify that fact. You understand that I have the regular procedures to carry through. What is Mr. Dobson's telephone number?"

"He won't be at the office this late," said Ted, so he gave the sergeant Mr. Dobson's home number rather reluctantly. Was it really necessary to bring him into this? Ted liked to feel that he could handle an assignment from the newspaper by himself, without having to run to Mr. Dobson for help.

The call went through. The boys got the impression that Mr. Dobson was giving them the strongest possible recommendation. Even the sergeant seemed impressed.

"Tell him we have no idea how the gun got into the car," Ted suggested, and the sergeant did so. Ted realized he would have to call Mr. Dobson later and explain more fully.

"You're acting on an anonymous telephone tip, aren't you?" Ted questioned.

"That's right. Personally I hate anonymous calls, but a police department can't afford to ignore them. By the way, you may as well sit down until we get the report on the gun."

As the sergeant turned to other work, the boys left the desk and sat down, puzzled and worried.

"When was the last time you looked in that glove compartment, Ted?"

"When I got the map out, on our way out here. What about you?"

"I haven't opened it at all. So when was it put in? The car was parked all night outside the coal mine. Then we parked at the motel, and this afternoon we walked to Phil's, leaving the car unguarded. It was in the parking lot tonight. What's your best guess? I'd say it was either last night or tonight. A person wouldn't be likely to fool around with a car in broad daylight."

"Tonight in the parking lot outside the Canteen seems the most likely. Last night nobody knew we were coming to East Walton, and certainly we never planned on parking all night outside the coal mine. Who knew we were there—unless you think this person just wanted to plant the gun on somebody, no matter who. Another point is that we *might* have gone into that glove compartment at any time, and if we found the gun we might have disposed of it quietly, or if we turned it in to the police, that would be a point in our favor. I think the person who planted the gun on us called the police almost immediately afterward."

"But what's the idea, Ted?"

"Oh, I don't think there's very much doubt about that," said Ted. "Somebody in town doesn't like what we're doing, and is trying to get rid of us."

"Trying to get rid of us? How?"

"If the police don't harass us enough to make us leave, maybe they hope Mr. Dobson will recall us, or maybe we'll scare out."

"Maybe number one or number two, but not number three," said Nelson emphatically. "I don't scare out, especially after somebody tries to pull something like this. But what are we doing that's hurting anybody?"

"We're going around asking questions. Apparently somebody doesn't like our questions, or at least is afraid of some of the answers we might get."

"Who knows that we've been going around town? We've only talked to maybe a dozen people."

"In a small town that's plenty. It's probably all over the place by now. Not that I think we're so important, but coal mining is certainly important to this town, and they'd want to know about anything that might help."

"Ted, there's only one way I can figure this. We're asking questions that will lead to a newspaper story, and might start an investigation that would lead to the reopening of the mine. Who could we be hurting? It has to be somebody who wants the mine to stay closed."

"Maybe," said Ted thoughtfully. "But what about the coal pirates, or anybody else who has committed some sort of crime? They might want the mine open, but still be afraid we would expose what they were doing."

"Everybody knows about the coal pirates, Ted."

"Yes—or thinks they do."

"What do you mean by that, Ted?"

"That there might be more going on in that mine than we realize. It might involve something more than just a question of stealing a few cartloads of coal every night."

Nelson began to count on his fingers: "Uranium, gold, pitchblende, diamonds . . . "

Ted smiled. "Or maybe just plain, everyday coal. Even coal's worth something, you know. I wonder how they work it? I don't know how many entrances there are to the mine. There must be miles and miles of tunnels underneath the ground there. I wonder if they could come all the way to East Walton? I suppose the idea was to build the city some distance away from the mine, so it wouldn't interfere with the mining, but it's possible the tunnels come close."

"I wish we were sitting above a tunnel right now, and I wouldn't care much if this police station fell right into it—after we're out of it. I wonder how much longer . . . "

As though in answer to his unfinished question, the patrolman returned to the room, and they followed him to the desk.

"No fingerprints," he told the sergeant. "But I've got the registered owner." He put a paper in front of the sergeant, who read it carefully, then turned to the boys.

"This is a stolen gun. It was taken in a burglary last night."

"The Royce drugstore?" asked Ted.

"Yes, you know about that?"

"We were over there this afternoon. Phil Royce is a correspondent for the *Town Crier.* He didn't say anything about a gun being stolen, though."

"No, I don't suppose he was eager to broadcast it. But he reported the theft to us. Since you know him, I'll ask him to come over. I have to tell him about the recovery of the gun, anyway."

He phoned the drugstore, and Phil promised to come over right away. The sergeant continued his questioning.

"Just for the record, where were you boys last night?"

"In the coal mine," Ted replied.

"The coal mine?"

"Say," said the patrolman suddenly, "these must be the boys who found the Llewellyn kids."

"That's right." The sergeant thumbed through some papers to verify it. "You fellows certainly did us a good turn."

The boys felt that the atmosphere was more cordial, even though the questioning continued.

"You say you were in the mine all night. Now of course that doesn't prove that you *couldn't* have robbed the drugstore. It's a pretty good alibi, but not a perfect one. If Phil Royce is willing to vouch for you, I guess that will be enough. Now if this gun was planted on you, as you claim, when was it probably done?"

"We were just discussing that," said Nelson, and went on to explain that it had probably happened at the parking lot near the Canteen.

"We'll check into it," the sergeant promised. "Do you usually keep your car locked?"

"Usually—in fact, just about always. But I wouldn't say the locks are so wonderful. Anybody with a string of car keys might be able to find one that would fit."

Phil arrived soon afterward. He admitted that this was the gun that had been taken in the robbery, but he was indignant that his friends should have been charged with the theft.

"I'm sure it was the work of juveniles, or at least somebody who was familiar with East Walton and the drugstore. These fellows are strangers here. They couldn't have known about the burglar alarm, and the rest of it."

"Have you known them very long?"

"Actually I never met either of them until this afternoon. But we've worked for the same newspaper for a long time. Ted's a responsible reporter, and he wouldn't be interested in a petty little robbery like this. To believe that he came all the way from Forestdale just to break into my store is ridiculous."

"Well, that makes sense," the sergeant agreed, "although I've heard about reporters who have done some pretty strange things for the sake of a newspaper yarn. I suppose, too, that there's a possibility that you somehow acquired the gun from the real burglars, just as there's a chance I might find a thousand dollars on my way home."

"Then are we cleared?" asked Nelson.

"I guess so—unless I find a thousand-dollar bill on my way home," he added. "Then I might decide to question you again."

"You can't say they mistreated us," Ted remarked when they got outside the station.

"Well, I'm glad to be out of there," Nelson added. "I'm not sure we would be, if it hadn't been for our alibi. We thought we helped the Llewellyn children, but it turned out that they helped us just as much."

"How was that?" asked Phil curiously.

"We spent last night together in the coal mine."

"You told me about finding the children, but you didn't tell me they had gone into the *mine*. That's a terribly dangerous thing for them to do. There ought to be a barricade to keep them out."

"I thought there was a kind of old barricade there," Nelson recollected.

"Very likely, but the men always tear them down."

"Yes, we've heard about the coal pirates," Ted explained.

"I knew you would before long. I don't suppose you could call it stealing, if the man you're stealing from knows about it and lets you do it. But they manage to keep the market busy—the black market, if you'll excuse the pun."

"Anyway, thanks for speaking up for us, Phil. If you ever come to Forestdale—"

"We'll bail *you* out," Nelson completed with a laugh. "Well, I spent last night in a coal mine, and almost spent tonight in jail. I wonder where I'll be sleeping tomorrow night?" And with that they broke up.

On the way back Ted stopped at an outdoor phone booth to call Mr. Dobson. He thought it better not to call from their cabin, where the call went through a switchboard. Mr. Dobson was anxious, as Ted knew he would be, to get fuller details on what had happened, and Ted brought him up to date on everything they had done in East Walton. He then told them to stick with the story and keep him informed.

Back in their cabin they reviewed the day's happenings.

"What burns me up, Ted, is that somebody planted that gun on us and is now probably laughing up his sleeve about it. Are we going to let him get away with it?"

"What do you think we ought to do?"

"Go back to the Canteen, and do a little checking up."

"The police are already following up that lead."

"And that'll get them a big fat nowhere. I imagine most of the young people in town drop in there regularly, and with all that confusion, it would be hard to remember who was there and who wasn't."

"Then what's your brainstorm?"

"Well, how about someone making sure of your attention while someone else planted the gun?"

"You mean Estelle? You're crazy."

"You're right, she *does* have attractive eyes," Nelson kidded. "OK. What's on tomorrow?"

"Mr. Winslow the first thing. And then I'm afraid that sometime or other we're going to have to go back into that mine. I can use the background material for my story. And as you say, we're not going to be scared off if we can help it. Then there's Alice. I'm still wondering where she could have wandered off to while the children thought she went into the mine."

"OK, Ted, I'm with you all the way. But you remind me a little bit of a man who walked a short way into quicksand, but didn't know for sure if it was quicksand, so he kept right on going to find out."

CHAPTER 8.

THAT MONSTER AUTOMATION

TED put through a call to Mr. Winslow, the president of the mining company, but found that he would not be available for an appointment until eleven o'clock.

"Then why don't we tackle someone else on your list, Ted? We could start right from the top with the mayor. Nobody could be higher than that."

Ted called the mayor's office, and was surprised at the answer. The mayor was neither at work nor at home, but perhaps could be found sitting in the park. The boys had already noticed the park, in the center of the small city, and drove to it.

They found him basking in the morning sun in his shirt sleeves. Though friendly, he did not rise to greet them, and they soon realized it was difficult for him to move around.

The mayor, upon learning that Ted was a reporter, was ready to get down to brass tacks.

"You young men know anything about figures?"

"He does." Nelson indicated Ted.

"Well, then," said the mayor, "let me tell you that that mine could be opened and worked at a profit, and I've got the figures to prove it."

"Did you ever show your figures to Mr. Winslow?"

"Of course I did. He disputes them, naturally. But my figures are reliable. They come from somebody who knows what he is talking about."

"I'm expecting to talk with Mr. Winslow this morning. Maybe he'll tell me what he thinks of your figures."

The mayor nodded. "He will. He'll weasel around them somehow. He wants to get paid for all the obsolete equipment he owns, and wants all his old debts paid off. Then, he'll tell you, maybe something could be done with these figures."

"When you speak about opening the mine again, are you talking about automation, or the old way?"

"I look upon automation as pretty much of a scare word, Ted. You're always going to need men, and maybe a great many men. You can invent a machine that can add better than you can, but what *else* can it do? The truth is it can't do anything at all until you tell it what to do. No machine has ever yet been invented that could decide *why* it ought to do something, or whether what it was doing was good or bad. But suppose fewer men are needed, if the change is made gradually no one need be hurt. As men retire or leave voluntarily, they simply won't be replaced."

"I've heard that argument before, and it doesn't convince me," Nelson said. "That way the older workers are protected, but young people can't find jobs because they aren't there to find."

"I don't think it's quite as bad as you suggest," said the mayor. "Young people can be educated for other jobs."

"I understand that it was a bad accident that led to the closing of the mine," Ted said.

"Yes, it was. As a young man I was a miner myself, so I'm not speaking as an outsider. I know what the risks are. I wouldn't tell you that it's the safest job in the world, but I think the risks have been exaggerated, too. You've heard about some of these big disasters. What do you think caused them? I don't care what the bosses say, or the unions say, or the legislators say, or the safety committees say. I can tell you what the miners say among themselves. They say that some miner sneaked off into a deserted pocket for a smoke, and touched off the accumulated gas."

"Do you think the miners are right?"

"It would be hard to prove it, but I'd be more inclined to take the word of a miner than that of anyone else. They're right at the root of the problem, and they know what's going on."

"Is it more dangerous for the coal pirates?" Ted inquired.

"Any time you have men working without supervision, it's dangerous. There's no one to enforce any standards upon them. Even under the best of circumstances it's always hard to enforce safety standards in a mine. The men are more interested in making money than they are in safety. But I will say that most miners, though they may be reckless about their own safety, try to protect their fellow workers."

"Wouldn't guards at the mine entrances put an end to the coal pirating?"

"Who knows how many entrances there are, after all these years, and who could afford full-time watchmen at each entrance? So the company puts up warning signs and erects barricades that are soon torn down, and hopes that that will be enough to keep them out of legal trouble. I suspect that it isn't enough, when it comes to small children too young to know what they're doing."

"Is there any way that Mr. Winslow could be forced to reopen the mine?"

"There are various ways of putting pressure on him. I think that Mr. Winslow is hoping too much for financial assistance. If he knew once and for all that he *wasn't* going to get any help from the state, he'd stop stalling around and figure out something else."

The boys had a chance a little later to compare the mayor's viewpoint with Mr. Winslow's. The mine president greeted them in a friendly manner.

"You're here because you want to know why the mine is closed, and what can be done about opening it again," he began. "Why else would you be here? It's the same question that's on everyone's mind, including my own."

"Are you the person who makes the decision?" Ted questioned.

"Yes, ultimately."

"What did you think of the figures that show the mine can be opened?" Ted went on.

"Very interesting, if you happen to like fairy stories. Do you know who prepared those figures? They were compiled by Mr. Patrick Sorrel. If you've been around town very much, you've heard about him."

The visitors nodded.

"He didn't publicly back up his figures, because he thinks the community is down on him. If I could start all over again, the mine could be operated competitively, just as he says. But how can I start over again? I'm hundreds of thousands of dollars in debt."

"What good are figures?" Nelson maintained. "Two people can take the same figures and come to exactly opposite opinions."

"It's a question of getting all the figures in, I suppose. If I could agree that all our equipment is obsolete, I might be won over to Mr. Sorrel's point of view."

"Isn't it true that your equipment is obsolete?" asked Ted.

"Of course, by automated standards, but that doesn't mean we have to scrap everything and start over. Here, let me show you something."

He took out a folder and showed them some pictures of a modern, automated mine. The cutting was done by huge machines that looked like monsters from outer space. Conveyor belts moved the coal out through brightly lighted tunnels. Everything was electrically powered, and the electricity in turn was probably generated by means of coal. Fifty years ago one man could produce about three tons of coal a day; today the production might be sixty tons, one man doing the work of twenty.

"It was an accident that closed the mine, I've heard," Ted said as he returned the folder.

"Yes, it did. The explosion made me realize that our safety standards were inadequate. I'm not a murderer, believe me. But I couldn't hire you to walk across the street for me and guarantee 100% safety."

"Mightn't there be some quite common and preventable cause of accidents?"

"You mean such as smoking in the mines? I'm afraid it's a much more complicated matter than that."

"You don't think this particular explosion was deliberately set?"

"Of course not, of course not. It's just a silly rumor. It's no wonder Mr. Sorrel grew bitter—and the people in East Walton don't even know how hard he tried to get the mines open, even to the point of writing a fairy story!"

"What about the coal pirates?"

"Oh, I know about them, of course, and I keep my eye on them. How much coal can you truck away in a night? But with practically no overhead, everything is profit."

"You heard about the Llewellyn children wandering into the mine?"

"Yes, and I'll put the barricade back up, but it won't keep older people out."

"Is it safe enough for anyone to go into the mine?"

"I turn on the air-conditioning equipment at intervals to keep poisonous gases from accumulating, and the water pumps have to be manned, and there are other ordinary maintenance measures."

"But no guards?"

"Our equipment is guarded, of course, but other than that I just couldn't do it. Nobody knows how far that mine reaches. There were dozens of tunnels made long before this company ever came on the scene."

Ted rose to his feet and Nelson followed his example. "I think we've taken enough of your time, Mr. Winslow, and I appreciate your help. Just one more question: what is being done about getting the mine back open?"

Mr. Winslow also rose. "I think the most honest answer I could give would be: nothing."

"And that's about the most honest answer I ever heard to anything," Nelson commented, as he and Ted walked toward the car. "Talk, talk, talk, and nothing is getting done, but our boy, Ted Wilford, comes along and thinks he's going to solve the whole problem."

"No, I don't," said Ted. "It's too big for me, and it makes me wonder if maybe it's too big for everyone."

"When are we going down in the mine again?"

"Let's make it tonight. Night or day, it's just as dark down there. But we can perhaps be a little more secretive about our plans, and if anybody else is up to anything, we might have a better chance of discovering it. And that'll give us time to make our preparations. Take along a little lunch, and make sure you've got plenty of fresh batteries.

It was agreed that they would spend the day on a few things that had been on their minds. Ted wanted to take a ride up to the railroad bridge crossing the river, to see if there was any likelihood that Alice had crossed there. They wanted to stop again at the Llewellyn farm. So far Nelson had not done much with his camera, until he had an idea what Ted wanted. But now that Ted's story was starting to take form in his mind, it was time for Nelson to get into action.

They left East Walton shortly after lunch, and some miles north arrived at the railroad crossing. The tracks crossed the highway in an overpass, and they parked the car to get out and look at it. It was with some difficulty that they climbed up the steep embankment.

"I don't think a mule could have made it," Nelson decided.

"No," Ted was obliged to agree, "unless Alice wanted to climb up the stone ledges, and I can't see her doing that. But is there an easier way?"

There didn't seem to be. There were fences along the right of way enclosing fields and pastures, which shut off any easy access. To get to the tracks, Alice would either have to jump a fence, or happen to find a gate open.

"More than one gate, Ted," Nelson pointed out. "She'd have to find her way through a regular network, and I'm sure Alice would be too smart to come all this way just on the slight chance of finding so many gates open."

They walked beside the tracks until they reached the river. The bridge crossing the river had large openings between the ties, which would probably have scared off any mule.

"They even scare *me*," Nelson observed.

"Well, then, I think we can consider it settled. Alice never came this way. I rather thought she might have, since Mr. Stevens mentioned this way as being shorter."

"Wouldn't that depend on just where Alice wanted to go on the other side of the river?"

"I suppose so, but she was found near West Walton. I'm glad Alice didn't try this bridge. There aren't as many trains, as there are cars, but even one would be too many."

They took a circuitous route back to the Llewellyn farm, bypassing East Walton but getting a good view of the countryside. The Llewellyn children were very glad to see them, and Nelson took a few pictures of them riding on the mule. Ted learned that there was a nearby pond at which Alice occasionally drank, but she was careful never to so much as wet a hoof. It was clear that she would never have voluntarily swum across the river. Even rain bothered her, and she would probably try to seek out some shelter.

"We can't be sure that Alice didn't take shelter in the mine," Nelson pointed out, after they had said goodbye to the Llewellyns and were heading back toward East Walton.

"No, except that if she waited out the storm in the mine, there would have been no time for her to get across the river after the storm was over."

Not wanting to waste what was left of the afternoon, Ted interviewed some more people on the list Mr. Allen had given him, while Nelson made preparations for their excursion to the mine, planned for late evening. Then about seven o'clock their telephone rang.

"This Ted Wilford?" asked a strange voice.

"Speaking."

"Do you want to know more about the coal pirates?"

"I'm certainly ready to listen."

"You can do more than listen. Be waiting for me in your cabin at ten o'clock—and wear some old clothes."

The caller hung up.

CHAPTER 9.

PIRATES AT WORK

WHEN Ted had relayed this conversation to Nelson, they stared at each other for a moment. Then Nelson threw down the knapsack he was packing. "This ends our own expedition, doesn't it?"

"I guess it does. It's a better lead than we could get by ourselves."

"What kind of lead, Ted? Just what good does it do us?"

"Well, we're anxious to find out everything we can about what's going on in the mine, right? And this is our chance to find out a little something."

"What are the pirates going to say if they catch us?"

"Let's hope they won't catch us. I doubt that the pirates will like the idea of anybody's spying on them."

"Except that everybody knows the pirating is going on," Nelson pointed out, "even Mr. Winslow. So what do the pirates care?"

"They might prefer not to be identified."

"That's easy, Ted. We don't know any of them well enough to identify them."

They spent a restless evening, waiting for the anonymous caller to show up. What if it were only something intended to interfere with their own plans? Or what if it had some sinister motive?

"Ted, suppose you did get a story, including the names of all the pirates and an exact description of what they were doing. What would you do with it? Print it, or do you happen to like the way you're put together?"

"I'm pretty well satisfied. But it wouldn't be up to me. Mr. Dobson would have to decide whether to use the story."

"And Mr. Dobson might have some qualms about getting you involved."

Ten o'clock came and passed, and they had about decided to give up on their visitor, when there came a discreet knock on their door. Nelson was closest, and opened it. There appeared to be no one there at first. Their visitor was standing off to the side.

"Ready to go?" he asked.

Nelson looked at Ted. "I guess we're ready. Will we take my car?"

"No, I've got mine a little way down the road. We'll go in that."

Ted left a note on his desk saying where they had gone—as far as they knew. Chances were it would do little good, but it was the only precaution he could think of that would not actually interfere with the story they were after.

The visitor walked on ahead of them. The car was parked in a dark spot, and they were unable to read the license plate. He motioned them into the front seat, then took his own place from the driver's side. He started the engine as quietly as he could, and the car moved slowly forward.

They could not tell much about their guide. Though he was not hiding his face, his hat was pulled low, and shadowed it. They got the impression that he was no older than they were. While it could not have been anyone they knew well, they were unable to eliminate the possibility it might be someone they had met briefly, perhaps at the Canteen.

"Where are we going?" asked Nelson, as much in the hope of drawing the young man into conversation as an attempt to pick up information.

The driver only shook his head, and refused to answer. Whether he was trying to hide his voice or whether he was simply worried they could not tell.

One thing seemed certain to the passengers: although they had expected right along that they were being taken to the mine, they could tell that they weren't going by the most direct route. Unfamiliar though they were with the roads around East Walton, it did not seem that they could circle around quite this much without getting anywhere. Apparently the idea was to confuse them, or to throw off anyone who might be following.

The driver's frequent glances in the mirror bore this out. After all, he couldn't be sure they hadn't told anyone about their excursion, and had arranged to have themselves followed.

They turned up some obscure side road, and after making several turns drew up to what was obviously an entrance to the mine. A truck was parked there—not a very large truck—and it was partly filled with coal. Their driver got out of the car, and motioned them ahead of him.

"How much coal do you think that truck would hold?" Ted asked Nelson in a whisper.

"About four tons, I'd say at a guess. If that's all they're able to haul away in a night, it's no wonder Mr. Winslow isn't interested."

Their guide had put a miner's light on his head, which helped to illuminate the path ahead of them. At the mine entrance he took the lead, while they followed close behind. They were following a set of tracks on which carts had once hauled coal.

The tracks branched off several times, but their guide seemed to know where he was going. If their guide should desert them, however, they would have no means of getting out except by feeling their way along the tracks. If they made a mistake and wandered up one of the branches, there was no telling where they might end up.

But a more immediate problem came to Ted's mind. He thought, once or twice, that he could hear the sound of shoveling or picking somewhere up ahead. How could their guide be sure that they would not accidentally stumble upon some of the pirates at work? That bright light would be a give-away, and could be seen a long distance up the tunnel ahead.

Ted wished they had brought a light of their own, but felt quite sure, somehow, that if they had, their guide would have taken it away from them before leading them into the mine. This must be a risk for him, and he wanted their full cooperation. Still it was awkward to be dependent upon a light held by someone else. They stumbled along after the young man, sometimes unable to avoid small obstacles that they could easily have stepped around with their own flashlights.

The picking seemed to be getting a little louder and closer. Wasn't it time for their guide to grow more cautious and urge them to be quiet and advance carefully? Suddenly he turned a corner, and as they followed him they saw several miners at work. They started to draw back, but their guide motioned them on, and announced to one of the men:

"Here they are."

Then at last Ted and Nelson tumbled to the truth. The guide wasn't a spy who wanted to expose the pirates. He was one of the pirates himself! It even seemed probable, from their attitude toward each other, that he was the son of the leader.

The chief of the coal pirates had a quiet voice and a pleasant manner.

"I take it that you are Ted Wilford, and you are Nelson Morgan," he began. "I know your names, of course, and I wish I could tell you mine. But I think we'll get on much better if I preserve our anonymity for the time being. If this is a newspaper story for you, you are welcome to your story, but not to our names."

"Do I understand that you brought us here so that I could interview you, and that you are willing to answer any questions apart from the names of your men?"

"That's it, Ted. You go right ahead."

Meanwhile, their former guide, his duty done, had drifted away, and the miners who had stopped work at their arrival now returned to their task. They were using picks and shovels, apparently the only tools they had. The little carts were loaded by hand, and when one of them was full, they saw one of the miners pushing it back down the tracks. Man power—even more primitive than mule power—and that was the way these men were earning a living! They suddenly realized how much a few dollars meant to these men, if they would work like this. Somewhere the boys heard a faint buzz, as though someone were idling the motor of either the truck or the car at the mine's entrance, but it soon stopped.

This was one of the most unusual interviews Ted had ever had. Just that day he had interviewed Mr. Winslow sitting before a broad desk in a neatly furnished office. Now the pirate leader was sitting on a large rock, seemingly glad of the chance to rest for a few minutes, and Ted and Nelson sat down, too.

"It would seem, sir, that you want me to print this story, since you went to quite a bit of trouble to get me here. What's your purpose in that?"

"Isn't it obvious? I don't particularly want our illegal activities publicized, but I think it just as well that people know as much as possible about how things are in East Walton. The more people we can interest in our case, the more likely it is that some sort of help will come to us. And of course there can't be any real benefits for any of us unless the mine reopens."

"Then you didn't trust me to find my own story?" asked Ted with a smile.

"I'll put it to you directly: you *couldn't* have got this story, if we didn't want you to have it. We have a small alarm system that would tell us when someone was coming, and we could disappear without your ever catching sight of us. And of course that is exactly what we would do, if an unauthorized person approached us. I know a little about you, Ted, and feel that you are a responsible reporter who will give us fair shakes in your story."

"Are you *really* afraid of being discovered," Nelson questioned, "when everyone knows you're here anyway?"

"They know *about* us, Nelson, but they don't know *us.* They don't know for sure who we are. Mr. Winslow could never give us *permission* to work in the mine the way we do. If he did, he would find himself in all kinds of trouble. But he pretends that he is unable to catch us and stop us, can't afford all the guards he would need, and so on. We, on our part, must pretend to be thieves, even though we know in our hearts that we are not. We are taking something that, for the time being, no one else wants, and won't be missed when the mine reopens. By helping our families, we are relieving a little of the burden on the public charities, and I suppose that people who buy our cheap coal are getting some small benefits, too."

"How many men do you have working here?" Ted inquired.

"I'd rather not mention any numbers, Ted, but I don't think I could give you any accurate figure, even if I wanted to. It isn't always the same number, and it isn't always the same men. Some nights there may be only two or three, some nights there are more. I suppose it depends on the state of a man's pocketbook whether he is willing to put in a night like this."

Nelson picked up the ax the miner had laid aside, and took a few swings at the face of the coal seam without making very much impression on it. If this was supposed to be soft coal, it still seemed hard enough to him.

"Whee! I thought I had muscles, but they seem to be the wrong kind of muscles for this work," he decided, putting the ax down again.

"Soft," said the miner with a slight smile visible behind the glare of his miner's lamp. Though he wasn't giving his name, he seemed to have little fear of being identified.

"Is this all you have," asked Ted, "just these hand tools?"

"That's all we can afford. Mr. Winslow has better equipment, of course, but he would never dare loan or rent it to us. Oh, I wouldn't say we wouldn't like a little better tooling, some power cutters, for example, but we make do with what we have."

"What about mules?" Nelson wanted to know.

"There used to be quite a few mules around. In fact, these tracks were designed for mule carts. But they were becoming obsolete, and when the mine closed the animals were all dispersed. I don't believe you'll ever find mules at work in this mine again. We would need better help than they could give to restore this mine to a competitive position."

"Then you do have hopes of this mine opening again?"

"It'll open, Ted, when enough people get together and decide that they want it open again. Your guess is just as good as mine about when that will be."

"If it reopened, would it be on an automated basis?"

"There would certainly have to be some big improvements made in the operation. But automation—I don't know just how far you'd have to go. If the mine were able to hire back only half the men who were laid off, that would still solve half our problem, wouldn't it?"

"What about safety? Isn't what you are doing sort of dangerous?"

"We don't let ourselves think about that, but accept whatever risks there are."

The interview ended then, and the miner summoned their former guide, who reappeared out of the shadows. Wordlessly, he led the way back along the tracks and out to the mine entrance. One or two cartloads of coal had been added to the truck while they were inside, and it was now about half filled.

They got into the car, and their guide, after circling around a little, returned them to the motel. He dropped them off a short distance from their door, then drove off, waving his hand.

"So those were the coal pirates," Nelson muttered. "You know, I think from now on I'll look at a dollar bill with a little more respect, now that I see what some people have to go through to earn it."

CHAPTER 10.

A PICTURE OF A GHOST

IN spite of being up till well after midnight, the boys were awake before eight the next morning.

"You know something, Ted? Just that little while we were down in the mine last night, and I could feel the coal dust sifting through my clothes and down my neck. If I hadn't had a long shower and a complete change of clothes, I'd feel dirty yet. Well, what's on the schedule for today?"

"I hope you don't feel too clean, because I wanted to follow our original plan to go down into the mine ourselves."

Nelson shrugged. "I'm willing, Ted, but why are we doing it? Didn't that visit last night help take care of that angle?"

"It helped, but I'd still like to do something on our own. And there's the matter of pictures, too. I'd like a few pictures taken inside the mine. We didn't have any chance last night."

"You won't get any pictures of workers in the mine, Ted."

"That's all right, as long as the mine's supposed to be closed anyway."

"We're after something more than pictures, aren't we?"

"I suppose we are. It's obvious that someone is trying to scare us out of town, and I'd like to know who and why. At first I thought it was the coal pirates, but that doesn't seem likely, after what they did for us last night."

"What about that? How does it rate as a newspaper story?"

Ted frowned. "I don't think it rates anything, at least right now. Mr. Dobson always says he wants us to get the story we're after, not the story people are ready to give us. Why do they want us to print this story, and how much of the truth are they really telling us?"

"Getting the mine reopened is a pretty good motive, isn't it?"

"I suppose it is. Well, I'll see how the whole thing fits together when I work on my long story. I won't use it now, though I want to call the office around eleven o'clock. We ought to be back by that time. I'm not really after anything much this morning, except to get our bearings."

"I thought the idea was to go at night," Nelson remarked.

"Sure, but that was because of the coal pirates. If we go into the mine at the entrance where we found the Llewellyn children, we'll be a long way from the coal pirates, don't you think?"

Nelson laughed. "You kidding?"

"Why?"

"You mean he really did get you lost last night? Here, if you want to know where we went, let me show you."

He spread his map out on the table, and traced a course with his pencil. It was not too easy a matter, for the unfinished roads were not shown on the map. But Nelson drew a line confidently, until he ended with a little circle.

"You'll find the entrance to the mine right around there, and I'm betting I'm not more than a small fraction of a mile off. You don't drive nearly as much as I do, Ted. If you did you'd notice little things that tell you where you are, and of course I've studied the map more, too."

"Next you'll be telling me you could even recognize the car."

"Of course," and Nelson reeled off a detailed description of it, which, for all Ted knew, might be completely accurate.

"How do you do that, Nel?"

"It isn't too hard. You notice the dashboard, and any other small points you can pick up. I admit I might be a year off on the age, though."

"It looks as though you're a better detective than I am," Ted complimented him.

"Maybe I'm better at noticing things, but you're better at putting the pieces together."

"I hoped I could recognize the driver if I saw him again. But after all, Nel, does it really matter if we recognize either the driver or the car? The important thing at the moment is that you seem to agree with me: the two entrances to the mine are miles apart."

They set out a short time later and soon arrived close to the spot where they had parked the car the first evening. Nelson asked whether there was any point in concealing the car.

"I think it might be a good idea to leave the car where it could be found easily," Ted pointed out. "If any kind of accident *did* happen, I'd like people to know where we went."

"There isn't going to be any accident if I can help it, Ted. Plenty of fresh bulbs and batteries," and he patted his pockets. Because Nelson had his camera to carry, Ted took the flashlight, and later went ahead as they entered the tunnel. Nelson had already taken two pictures, the first a distant shot of the entrance, and the second a closer view.

It was with a slightly eerie feeling that the boys took the same course they had followed as they searched for the Llewellyn children.

"Just think that I'm exploring a dirty old coal mine on a bright summer morning, for some strange reason I can't begin to understand," Nelson remarked. "But there's one thing I *do* understand all right, Ted—I don't intend to get lost. What about you?"

"I don't plan to get lost either. In fact, I'm starting right now to make a sketch of the path we came along," and taking out his notebook Ted suited his actions to his words. "What's your contribution to the cause?"

"I've got some pieces of chalk in my pocket, and I'm going to mark every turn we take on the dark wall surface. And where the walls are too light to show the chalk, I'm going to use coal as a marker instead."

"I can't think of much more we could do then, unless you want to sprinkle bread crumbs after us."

They reached the point of the first turnoff, where they had eventually found the Llewellyn children, and now the same decision faced them. Nelson once more maintained that the turn to the left looked like the best course, and urged that they take it. Ted, still figuring it was a tossup either way, once more agreed. He brought his map up to date as accurately as he could, even estimating the number of feet he thought they had descended below the entrance. Nelson did his part by drawing a large arrow in the required direction, with both the date and his initials.

"How about the time?" Ted said with a laugh, but Nelson thought this was a good idea, and added it.

They were now in the same room from which they had turned back on their first visit. Ted flashed the light all around, but there wasn't much to see. Although this area had been mined at one time, there was no sign of recent activity as far as they could tell. There were no fresh scars, no tools around, not even a sense of loose dust, and the path looked solidly worn. They crossed to the opposite doorway of the room, and went on into another room, much like the one they had just left. The one exception was that this room had two additional outlets, so Ted brought his map up to date while Nelson made his markings once more, indicating the door they decided to follow.

This door did not lead directly into another room, but into a long tunnel. They followed the tunnel for a while, but soon found there were numerous turnoffs. Following two or three of these, they discovered they were dead ends, and soon returned to the main corridor. There were dozens of these side paths, and they wondered whether there was any point in trying to follow them all.

"It seems to me, Ted, that these are probes, which tested whether the coal was good enough and there was enough of it to justify larger operations. I guess they turned out to be minor leads, and so they were abandoned. What do we do? Are you anxious to make as complete a map of the mine as possible?"

"That was sort of my idea, but I can see that we're not going to be able to do it in a few days. It's a little like hunting for a needle in a haystack."

"And we aren't even sure that it's a needle we're hunting for," Nelson concluded.

Ted did not want to abandon the side paths entirely, but felt they could save time if only one of them went in to explore these smaller tunnels, while the other stood outside on the main corridor. They took turns, without finding any thing of interest, and whenever one of them returned from such a fruitless side expedition, Ted showed the corridor as a broken line on his map, while Nelson put a large "D.D." in chalk on the wall at the entrance.

"That stands for dead end," he claimed, and when Ted asked about his choice of initials, he explained, "the first and the last letters. What's wrong with that?"

"Nothing, only I thought maybe it stood for Donald Duck."

But soon they came to a corridor that promised something more interesting. Ted came part way back and called to Nelson:

"Come on, this seems to go on and on."

Nelson joined him, after marking his usual notations at the entrance while Ted brought his map up to date. The tunnel they were now following, smaller than the main corridor, took several turnings, which Ted noted as carefully as he could. It was downhill; they were gradually getting deeper and deeper into the mine. The tunnel eventually widened out into a small room, which in turn led them into a larger room. Here they came across the first really interesting thing.

"Recent digging," said Ted, picking up a handful of loose dirt that had not been packed down. "But that's dirt, not coal."

"Maybe some coal, too." Ted flashed the light along one of the walls, and there were a number of gashes in it. There might have been no way for them to guess how old these gashes were, except that there was a scent of coal dust in the air, fresh dust that had had no time to settle.

"If this is real coal-mining territory, then I think it's the place for a picture," Nelson decided.

He set up his camera near the entrance to the large room, the biggest they had yet seen in the mine, Ted thought, as he flashed his light about casually along the walls and roof.

"How much can you get with a flash bulb?" he questioned.

"Not too much," Nelson admitted. "The light from the bulb has to travel *to* the subject, and then back again to the camera, so everything gets pretty faint when you get very far away. But I ought to be able to catch something, at least enough to suggest what a coal mine looks like from the inside."

The flash went off, temporarily blurring their vision. Then Nelson took another picture from the same spot, but turning a little more to one side.

"What now, Ted? Do we go on?"

Ted looked at his wristwatch, noting that already a little layer of coal dust had settled behind it.

"We don't have too much time if I'm going to telephone at eleven. And another thing—do you know where we are?"

"You're the map-maker. You ought to know."

"Well, if my calculations are anywhere near right, we're almost directly below the room we first entered. We're on a different level entirely, and there's no telling how many other levels there are below us. When I thought about map-making, it didn't occur to me that I'd have to make the map in three dimensions. Just to be careful, I'm not sure we ought to go on. I don't want to get mixed up."

Being a little pressed for time, and anxious to check whether they had taken enough safeguards to keep from getting lost, they retraced their steps. Nelson took several more pictures along the way, Ted appearing in some of them. These pictures, while possibly of little use for Ted's story, would help remind them later of what it had felt like to explore a coal mine.

Retracing, they found that both Nelson's markings and Ted's map were useful. Nevertheless, they were glad to find themselves once more back in the room where they had started. Not long afterward, they saw the bright sunshine through the mouth of the mine.

Back at their cabin, while Nelson cleaned up, Ted made a few notes preparatory to calling the *Town Crier.* Before he was finished, the phone rang.

"Ted?"

"Speaking."

"This is Phil Royce. This is your deadline morning, isn't it?"

"Yes, I was just about to call the office."

"I thought you would be, and I tried reaching you a little while ago, but you weren't in. I don't have very much, Ted, but here's one small item if you want it. Doctor James Clifford is moving to a new address. He has been living out of town, but now wants to move into town to be nearer his work. His new address is 3823 Western Avenue. Got that? He's pretty prominent in town, so it might be of some use."

"I'll call it in, Phil. Mr. Dobson may use it, depending on how his space is running. Anything else?"

"No, not now. See you, Ted."

Ted then called the paper. Mr. Dobson had some questions about Ted's activities, but did not intend to use anything about the mine until he had Ted's complete story. He made a note of the small filler, however, and thought he might squeeze it in.

"How do we stand, Ted?" asked Nelson, emerging from the bath-room in fresh clothes. "Did we explore that mine well enough—I mean, even for a beginning?"

Ted shook his head. "Not even much of a beginning, I'm afraid. Remember that second room we went into? There were two exits, and we only took one. Then we didn't even follow through on the main corridor, but took the side path that led us below, and when we came to that big room, we quit. That's what we did with our first *left* turn. We didn't even try the right turn. I'd say we didn't get very far."

"Do we go back, then?"

"Maybe sometime. Let's see what develops first."

"Develops—anything wrong if I start on my pictures, Ted? I'd like to see what I've got."

"OK, but if you're going to use the bathroom for a darkroom, let me shower first."

When Ted had finished, Nelson arranged a blanket over the bath-room window, and set to work with his developer, while Ted took their clothes to the laundromat. Then they had lunch.

"I'll print the pictures when I get a chance, Ted. I don't have my enlarger along, but I can make contact prints."

They stopped in at the drugstore, and Ted thanked Phil for his morning call.

Phil looked perplexed. "What call do you mean, Ted?"

"Don't you remember? You called me about Doctor Clifford this morning."

"What are you talking about, Ted? I didn't call you. I had a few items that I sent in by mail yesterday."

"Well, then, what's going on? Did Doctor Clifford move?"

"Not that I know about."

If this was a practical joke, it seemed so pointless they were un-able to understand it, until Phil asked Ted to tell him exactly what the caller said. Then Phil laughed.

"I hate to tell you this, Ted, but that address—it's the local cem-etery!"

"And I mentioned the doctor wanted to be near his work? Oh, boy!"

"That doesn't sound so bad," Nelson said. "Anybody can make a mistake on an address, and no one outside of East Walton will even recognize it."

Ted felt obliged to correct him. "Don't kid yourself, Nelson. This is one of those little items the big papers like to pick up, to ridicule the country papers. It'll be all over the state before the week is over."

"It won't have your name on it, will it?"

"No, but everybody will be sure to give credit to the *Town Crier*."

"What will Mr. Dobson say?"

"Nothing—and that's what's going to make it all the worse."

Phil had already guessed they had gone exploring in the coal mine that morning, and they felt it was useless to deny it. Then Phil, who said he could take a little time off that afternoon, suggested some tennis, and they were glad to agree.

After about forty-five minutes on the court, Phil said he must return to the drugstore to see if his father was caught in the flash of trade that sometimes developed. He promised to return as soon as he could, but when their set was finished they decided not to wait.

"I guess we're really supposed to be working," Ted remarked, and Nelson reluctantly agreed with him. They stopped at the drugstore to pick up their coats, which they tossed into the car, said good-bye to Phil, and returned to their cabin. Ted decided he should begin to get his story down on paper while it was still fresh in his mind, and Nelson wanted to print pictures. While they were both so engaged, Phil called to say that Ted had dropped his notebook over at the drugstore, and since he couldn't get away just then, promised to hold it for him. Phil's voice, Ted noticed, wasn't quite like the voice he had heard on the phone that morning, but there was a similarity, as though the early caller had been trying to imitate Phil.

Then Nelson called from the bathroom. "Hey, Ted! Did you think we were alone in that mine this morning?"

"As far as I knew we were."

"Well, don't fool yourself. There's something on one of the pictures. How would you like to see a ghost?"

CHAPTER 11.

BY MOONLIGHT

THERE was nothing on the picture Nelson handed to Ted that looked at all like a ghost. It was a picture taken inside the mine, with a dark background in the manner of flash pictures, and perhaps for that reason slightly sinister.

"I don't see any ghost," said Ted, wondering what Nelson had in mind.

"Of course you don't. Everybody knows you can't see ghosts. But you can tell when they're around. What do you see?"

Ted examined the still-damp picture more carefully. He did see something, or perhaps several things. Most prominent was a pickax standing against the wall, which he certainly hadn't noticed when they were in the mine.

"Let's get oriented. Where was this picture taken?"

They had to check with all of Nelson's negatives before they felt sure. Then they agreed that it was taken in the large room, their turn-around point. Nelson had taken another exposure in the same room, but this one did not show the pickax, for he had pointed his camera in a slightly different direction.

"As I remember, Ted, you were flashing the light all around the room, the ceiling, walls, and floor, to get an idea of what it was like. You didn't happen to focus on the opposite wall, or even if you did the flashlight wouldn't carry as well as the flash bulbs."

"That pickax might have been left there any time. It doesn't prove anything."

"No, but what about the rest of it?"

Ted looked at the picture once more. There were certainly a number of other items lying around.

"Is that a coat draped on the ledge?"

"That's what it looks like, and maybe a hat beside it—it's hard to tell. What do you see on the ground?"

"Hmm,—it might be a box. At first I thought it was a rock, but the sides seem too regular."

"Yes, that's what it is—an orange-colored box."

Ted studied the black-and-white picture. "How can you tell it's orange?"

Nelson shrugged. "I just know it's orange, that's all. There's no way I can explain it to you. If you're familiar enough with your camera and your film and your lighting and your distance, then you know how orange will look."

"What shade of orange is it?"

"A bright orange—just about the brightest you can imagine."

"Well, I suppose orange is a good color for something you are going to take down in a coal mine with you. It looks like a metal box to me. That would be useful for keeping the coal dust out. I wonder if the box contained instruments of some kind?"

"No telling, Ted. What do you think of our ghost now? Did he just vanish into thin air, the way a ghost is supposed to do?"

"More likely we surprised him and he got out of there fast with his light, not even taking time to gather up his equipment. I wish I knew what was in that box. Too bad we didn't notice it at the time."

"Want to go back, Ted?"

"What's the use? He's come back for his box and gone by now. I wonder who it could be?"

"How about a maintenance man," Nelson suggested, "or maybe one of the coal pirates?"

"I don't think a maintenance man would run from us. He'd be more likely to step up and demand to know what *we* were doing there. But I don't think it's a coal pirate, either. We were a long way from the place the pirates were working last night."

"Unless there is more than one crew of them," Nelson pointed out. "Who knows what's going on in that underground circus?"

"Even so, the pirates usually work as a group, not alone, and the pirating is usually carried on at night, to keep up the pretense that nobody knows about it."

"Then what was he doing in there?"

"That's a good question. Maybe he's just as innocent as we are—wanted to explore the mine but couldn't get permission."

"Only we didn't explore with a pickax," Nelson pointed out. "He was digging. What's that mean, Ted? Has he discovered something valuable?"

"Who knows? It could be anything, from simple curiosity to a—a secret diamond mine. They're both carbon, anyway."

They went out for an early dinner and noticed Mr. Sorrel sitting alone at a table when they entered the restaurant. He nodded at them but made no move to invite them over.

"Want to go over and talk with him, Ted?" asked Nelson.

"I suppose so. I've wanted to talk to him again, and this may be as good an opportunity as any." They walked across the room. "Mind if we join you?" Ted inquired.

"Why should I mind?"

This was as cordial an invitation as they could expect, and they sat down at the table, all three giving their orders to a waitress.

"At least I know who you are this time," Mr. Sorrel began abruptly, "and by now I'm sure you've heard all the gossip about me."

"Maybe not all of it," said Nelson.

"Enough, then. Aren't you afraid to eat with a man who would blow up a coal mine just because he *might* make a little extra money out of it?"

"I haven't uncovered any proof that you did it," Ted assured him, "and it doesn't sound very probable to me. I don't know what they have to base their suspicions on."

"It's my personality. A person who isn't just like everybody else, and especially one who doesn't even want to be, is always suspect. If you're trying to feel me out for my side of the story, Ted," Mr. Sorrel continued, "I haven't any. I'm not going to admit I touched off the explosion, and I'm not going to deny it. If I were capable of a thing like that, I'd surely have no scruples over lying about it. And there's no use saying I didn't do it, because people are going to believe what they want to anyway."

"I talked with Mr. Winslow about the figures you gave him," Ted went on. "He was quite critical of them."

"Naturally. Other businesses, when they become outmoded, have to accept their losses, but Mr. Winslow feels he should somehow be an exception. He may be successful, too, if he can get enough people to make a big enough squawk to the legislature. That's what he's leading up to with you, isn't it?"

Ted hadn't thought of it that way before. Certainly, Mr. Winslow had not even mentioned the legislature, but it might have been in his mind. That was reckoning without Mr. Dobson, however; the latter refused to represent anyone's opinion except his own.

"If he was, he was wasting his time."

Their food was served, and Mr. Sorrel, after remarking to the waitress about the delay, complained to her about his food, though the boys found everything very good. And then, as he departed, he left an extraordinarily large tip for the waitress. How could you ever understand a man like that, the boys wondered.

"Did he do it or didn't he, Ted?"

"Oh, I'm beginning to believe more and more that it was an accident. But just saying that doesn't help Mr. Sorrel much."

"If you want to help a man who carries a gun in his car," and Ted looked at Nelson sharply. Could that have been the reason Mr. Sorrel was so careful to lock his car?

Back at their cabin, Nelson asked how Ted's story was coming.

"I have a pretty good idea what I want to say. The problem is saying it. I want to use a great many quotations, and it's important that I quote people just as accurately as I can."

"Does this include the anonymous captain of the coal pirates?"

Ted frowned. "Yes, perhaps him most of all. The others can correct me if I give a wrong impression, but he probably wouldn't want to come forward. Nel, let's take a good, hard look at what happened last night. How many men did we see in the mine?"

"Five, all together, counting our guide. But it seemed to me that there were probably other men around that we *didn't* see."

"Yes, I got that impression, too. Now when we arrived at the entrance to the mine, how many cars were there?"

"No cars, except the one we came in. But there was that truck."

"Yes, and I suppose that everyone could have come in the truck. But somehow I can't picture a coal truck going around East Walton and picking up all the workers."

"They may have come by private cars, and hidden them. They wouldn't want them left out where everyone could see them, would they?"

"The truck was left out in plain sight," Ted pointed out, "and our guide didn't make any effort to hide *his* car. How much secrecy would they want, and why? I'm thinking if some of the other cars were hidden, there might be a good reason for it. They might not want Mr. Winslow to know just how much pirating was really going on."

"The number of cars wouldn't necessarily give that away," Nelson remarked. "There would be no way to tell whether a car carried one man or six or eight, though you wouldn't exactly want a whole parking lot full of cars sitting around. But that's not the main point, Ted. More important than the number of cars would be the number of trucks to haul the coal away, and we only saw one. I don't see much point in having many more than one, at the slow rate they were able to load that one up."

"All right, then. Maybe the cars weren't hidden, and the reason we didn't see them was because they weren't there. Isn't it possible that that wasn't the only entrance they were using? Maybe the cars were parked closer to a different entrance, where mining was going on at a larger scale."

"You mean, Ted, that maybe everything we saw last night was just a show they were putting on for our benefit?"

"Maybe not so much for our benefit, as for Mr. Winslow's. But after we got on their trail, it may have seemed a good idea to put on the same show for us. Invite us in and *show* us what's happening, so we won't be tempted to snoop around and perhaps discover something that we weren't supposed to."

Suddenly Nelson stood bolt upright. "Ted, now that you've got me thinking that way, there was something else that was suspicious, too. You remember we heard a little humming sound? I thought at the time it might be from one of the car motors. But when we got back, no one had touched the car, and the truck was still there so apparently it hadn't been moved. And now that I think of it, I believe we were too far away from the entrance to hear them, anyway. After we heard the humming, our guide slipped away, and then it stopped. They must not have realized we would be able to hear it there."

"You're the mechanic. Tell me what we heard."

"It could have been a generator, Ted. They may have electricity in there, and power tools, maybe even electric carts and loaders, and goodness knows what all. Maybe they're making a big thing of it." Then he shook his head. "No, there's one thing wrong with the picture. They don't have the trucks. I'm sure they couldn't have dozens of trucks on the highways every night without Mr. Winslow's hearing about it."

But as Nelson's face grew longer, Ted became excited. "I think you're right about that, Nel. Now let's look at this spot you drew on the map. You still think it's accurate?"

"It should be pretty close."

"All right, then. Do you notice anything in particular about it?"

Nelson studied the map for a minute, but finally shook his head. "Can't say I do."

"Well, it's not very far from the river, is it? We were just a little east of the highway. Suppose the mine tunnels under the road and through those low hills—and there you are at the river. I'm sure that a motor barge could haul a good deal more than the four tons the truck could hold."

"It would be a dangerous operation, Ted," Nelson objected. "So many things could go wrong."

"But desperate men might be willing to take the risk. If Mr. Winslow allows them to operate, and it turns out to be a larger operation than he suspected, that doesn't put him in a very sound legal position."

"Ted, I think you've got something. And to think of all the pity I wasted on those poor miners last night. How much do you suppose they make?"

"A good deal more than they let us think. And it's as Mr. Winslow says: forget all about safety and overhead. If they aren't actually 'borrowing' his equipment, I'll bet they're at least using his tracks and supports and relying on his air conditioning and pumps. They're probably overlooking a small detail called income tax. Save a little of your pity, though, Nel. It is hard work, and it's dangerous in two ways—you might get blown up or you might get caught. Certainly it's nothing you can build your future on."

"You may have a good story there, Ted, but how do we prove it?"

"By observation, I guess. We'll scout around tonight to see if there really is a barge, or whether I dreamed up the whole thing."

With a few hours to spare, Nelson suggested that they drop in at the Canteen. He still was unwilling to forget about the gun planted on him.

"All right, Nel, but what sort of clue do you expect to find?"

"Maybe nothing more than a guilty look—something like that."

"It's pretty doubtful that anyone who would do that would feel guilty about it."

"Just the same I'd like to know who it was that introduced you to Estelle, Ted. Don't you remember who it was?"

"No, someone just took my arm, and there I was. If she's there tonight, I'll ask her."

They were fortunate to find Estelle was there. It was between dances, and she came over toward Ted as soon as she saw him.

"Nice to see you again, Estelle," Ted said. "Say, how about settling a bet between Nelson and me over who introduced us. Do you remember?"

"Come on, I'll show you." She led him to the opposite side of the room, Nelson following a little behind. "Ted, I want you to meet Jerry Jansen," and suddenly Ted found himself staring straight into the eyes of the pirate captain's son.

They shook hands mechanically as they stared at each other. Had Ted given away the fact that he recognized their guide? He didn't know, but he was afraid that he had. Then the music began, and he turned away, realizing that Estelle had taken it for granted he was to dance with her.

"You see," she went on to explain, "I heard who you were, and told Jerry I wanted to meet you, so he got hold of you, even though he hadn't met you himself. It was supposed to be my dance with him, but he sat there and watched us the whole time instead. Wasn't that nice of him?"

"Very generous, I'm sure. He keeps sort of late hours, doesn't he?"

She looked up at him. "Then you do know about it? My parents don't approve of him because of that, but I don't think he can help it. He wouldn't do it if there was any other choice. Don't you think so, Ted?"

"He seems to be a fine young man. I'm not quite sure just what standards are acceptable around here."

"Ted, I really did enjoy our dance the other night, but I wasn't quite honest, either. I wanted to find out how much you knew about things, and then, maybe, to ask you for a promise."

"What promise, Estelle?"

"That no matter what happens, you won't use his name in a newspaper story."

"Unless he's arrested, I promise not to use his name, Estelle. That's our usual policy anyway."

"Thanks, Ted. You've relieved my mind." And Estelle gave him a big smile.

"Did you recognize Jerry?" Ted asked Nelson later.

"Not until I saw from your attitude that something was wrong. Then I caught on. Think maybe he planted the gun on us, Ted?"

"Estelle gives him an alibi. She says he was watching us the whole time we were dancing."

"And I know better than to suggest they were in it together," said Nelson with a laugh. "I didn't do any better myself—not a guilty look anywhere."

It was ten-thirty as they set out, Nelson first checking the glove compartment in his car, but finding nothing unexpected. Though they went by car, they dared not approach too close to the mine or one of its many undisclosed entrances. Instead they parked in a secluded spot they felt was well beyond the area of the pirates' operations. Leaving the car, they climbed one of the low hills that lined the east bank of the river. The moon was bright that night, and they were careful to keep in the shadows as much as they could. Upon reaching the river bank, they began to work their way northward, back toward the mine.

"Of course we don't know that the barge will come tonight, even if there is a barge," Nelson observed.

"In that case, we'll keep coming back every night till we do find it, or are convinced there isn't any such thing."

"How long is it going to take to convince us?"

But that was a question Ted could not answer. He knew that a paper the size of the *Town Crier* could not afford to keep him out on a story like this for long, no matter how good the story looked. But he knew that he had Mr. Dobson's confidence and understanding, and he hoped that something would break soon. Meanwhile he was keeping his expenses to a minimum.

It was not easy going, even by the light of the first-quarter moon. Already the moon was approaching the western horizon. When it set, it would be harder. But then, Ted thought, that might be exactly what the pirates were waiting for.

They had walked quite some distance, when Nelson suggested, "Why don't we climb part way up one of these hills, and hide there? It would give us a pretty good view of the sweep of the river. We don't actually have to be sitting in their laps in order to know what goes. In fact, I'd much prefer not to get too close. Those pirates were awfully friendly last night, when they were showing us what they wanted us to see. They're going to be a good deal less friendly if we see something they don't want us to."

Ted agreed that a certain amount of caution represented the better part of valor, and they climbed till they found a suitable spot. There they took their places in the silent night. The dark river swept past them with only the faintest of ripples; a few fireflies were still out; from time to time a bat or nighthawk glided noiselessly overhead. The stars were bright in a cloudless sky, but the moon would be setting soon.

Almost as the moon set, as though by pre-arranged signal, a big black hulk, visible only as a silhouette against the lighter shore, came into view from around the bend some miles upstream. They could hear no sound of engines as it drifted over toward the eastern shore and was made fast in an incredibly short time.

"So they really are pirates," Nelson whispered, although there seemed no need for such exaggerated quiet. "I thought that was a queer name for them, but when they take to the water, I guess the name is just right."

Ted was happy that a boat that had existed only theoretically had turned out to be real.

There was little chance of discovery from the opposite shore, sparsely inhabited with woodland and marshes reaching down to the water's edge at that particular point. If the boat were seen, it might never be reported because it would be assumed there was a little legitimate mining going on.

"But what about the boat, Ted? You can't hope to hide a big thing like that on a river."

"They might not have any reason to hide. Once they've pulled away from the shore and got a mile or so downstream, they may turn on their lights again and act as though everything is all right. There still are mines open, farther up the river, and the boat might be coming from there, as far as most people could tell."

"Except for speeding or jaywalking, I don't remember ever seeing a crime committed before, Ted. What should we do?"

"I'll have to tell the story. Let other people catch the criminals. I certainly don't know their names or exactly where they live."

"Shouldn't we report this to Mr. Winslow?"

"His interests might be exactly the opposite of mine. Oh, I suppose he'd stop the operation, but he wouldn't like the idea of publicity, either. He'd suppress the story if he could, but he isn't going to have the chance."

"One thing gets me, Ted. Why *doesn't* Mr. Winslow know about this operation? He couldn't be in with the pirates, could he?"

"I shouldn't think so. I imagine it would be small potatoes to him. It must be that he doesn't know about it because he doesn't think it's possible. He was never given the benefit of a personally conducted tour by a pirate captain, and just happened to hear the hum of a generator in the background."

They were too far away to tell what methods were being used to load the barge, but it was being done with speed. Long before the first gray streaks of dawn, the job was finished, and the barge was silently caught up in the currents in midstream, passed the onlookers by, and disappeared around a bend below.

Nelson stood up. "Don't you feel like somebody's watching us, Ted?"

"Yes, dozens of people. Let's get out of here before we get caught by daylight."

Somehow feeling guilty for having seen something they weren't supposed to see, they returned to the car, and drove back to the cabin.

CHAPTER 12.

WHAT HAPPENED?

AT least we didn't let the pirates buffalo us, Ted," said Nelson with grim satisfaction next morning as they got a late start.

But Ted didn't have much to say about the story. He was still too busy planning it in his mind. The pirating was a good story and a big one, but it still wasn't the whole story by any means. Quite a number of other problems puzzled him: where Alice had spent that first night, which might be merely a matter of curiosity but could on the other hand hold some deep significance for them; whether the Llewellyn children were menaced; who planted the gun on them and made the fake telephone call; who was the ghost in the mine; and perhaps most important of all, how could all the opinions about the mine and its situation be somehow reconciled, so that everyone would work for the reopening of the mine?

He replied, in answer to a question from Nelson, that he really did believe that the same person had planted the gun and made the call, or perhaps the same group of persons, if there was some organized plot to get them out of town.

"And I'm pretty sure it isn't the coal pirates, Nel. For all they know, we're still on their side. We won't have any trouble with them unless they catch us nosing around too much—or until my story appears."

"I'm glad it wasn't Jerry. I thought he was kind of nervous, but I guess that's natural, knowing what he did about the real operations there. But the chief didn't seem upset at all. It just goes to show you."

"Whoever made that call would have to know quite a bit about my work here, and the *Town Crier,* and our deadlines. He had to call almost at the last minute, for otherwise I might be in contact with Phil and realize the story was a fake."

"I don't think it would be much of a problem to find out about your deadlines, Ted. Phil's probably been going around town for years, telling people, 'Be sure to let me know before eleven o'clock. That's my deadline time.' "

"Well, yes, I suppose anyone could know, if he wanted to," Ted conceded.

They stopped first at the drugstore to pick up Ted's notebook. Phil had a copy of that morning's *Town Crier,* and showed them the story about the doctor. It was a small item, tucked down at the bottom of the front page. "Just where people are most likely to see it," said Ted with a groan.

Since Phil was busy, they went off for a combination breakfast-lunch at a cafeteria. Then they decided to take a walk through the park. Afterward they both claimed they saw it first: a man sitting on a park bench quietly eating his lunch from a metal box colored the brightest orange they had ever seen!

"Hey!" Nelson exclaimed involuntarily.

"Take it easy. That's probably not the only orange-colored lunch box in town."

"But what a shade of orange, Ted—brilliant, just the way I told you. What were we saying about having some important instruments in there? What can be more important than food?"

They walked past the man, looking at him casually, but well enough so they felt confident of recognizing him again. Then they sat down on another bench at a little distance.

"Are we going to try to identify him, Ted?"

"I'd like to. I wonder if he walked or drove here?"

"Probably left his car in the parking lot and walked over here, just the way we did. We could wait till he leaves and then see which car is his."

"Yes, but that might be too late to get his license number."

"Don't worry, if I get a good look at the car I'll be able to recognize it again. Meanwhile, I've got a bag of peanuts and we can sit here and feed the squirrels."

"I don't see any squirrels."

"Haven't you got any imagination?"

But they did not have a very long wait. When the man had finished his lunch, he put everything away carefully, and sauntered toward the parking lot. The boys followed at a little distance, but the man never glanced behind him, and seemed not to notice them at all. Apparently he merely wanted to get something out of his car, and having done so, he walked off again, leaving the lunch box behind him. There was no trouble at all about getting the license number.

"Well, we did it," Nelson gloated, clapping his hands with satisfaction.

"Did what?"

"Identified the ghost."

"All I've got here is a license number of somebody who *might* be the ghost."

"Well, isn't that enough? Or should we wait around and try to follow him?"

"No, I don't think it would do much good. I don't believe he has any intention of going back to the mine today, judging by the clothes he's wearing. And if he's staying at the hotel, or with friends in town, what good does it do us?"

"At least we can find out his name now."

"Do you want to go to the police and ask them?"

"No," Nelson decided, recollecting certain circumstances.

"I don't either. But I think if I put through a call to Forestdale, Sergeant Jeffers might be willing to help out."

Ted put through the call, and Sergeant Jeffers said he would oblige. Getting the man's name would take only a few minutes, but if Ted wanted more information about him, that would take longer. Ted decided that the name wouldn't help much unless he knew a little more about the man.

"I'll call you back later in the day, because you might have trouble reaching me here. Thank you, Sergeant."

Ted had at least two more people he wanted to interview from Mr. Allen's list, plus some others besides, and it was time for Nelson to begin taking some pictures of the people Ted intended to quote in his article. Expecting that they would proceed with this assignment, Nelson was surprised when Ted hesitated.

"I wonder, Nel, if this wouldn't be a good time for us to go back down in the mine."

"Why now, Ted?"

"Because we're pretty sure our ghost *isn't* there, and I'd just as soon not run into him again below ground."

"You mean we'll try to find out what he was up to?" asked Nelson.

"No, I don't have much hope of that, at least until I hear from Sergeant Jeffers. Probably all we'd see would be a few places where he was digging, and it wouldn't mean anything to us. But I want to get a little better acquainted with that mine, and this time I want to turn *right.*"

"Hey, you're getting as stubborn as Alice," said Nelson with a laugh, but he agreed with Ted's idea. They had begun to get a notion of what the mine was like along the left turn, so why not try the other one?

It was decided that Nelson would not carry his camera this time, for he had already taken a number of pictures there, and he had little hope of finding another ghost. If they encountered anything strange perhaps they could come back at a later time for the picture. The main reason for leaving the camera behind was that they had found it awkward to have only one flashlight. It would be much better for each of them to carry a light.

"Then if a flashlight burns out, at least we won't have to change it in the dark," Nelson remarked, "although my logic teacher might point out that they could both burn out at the same instant."

"We'll chance that," Ted decided.

They bought another flashlight, and after making sure they had plenty of replacement lights and batteries, they set out on their fourth journey into the mine. And although Ted had no clear idea what he was after, he was resolved that this was going to be their deepest and most thorough penetration. His notebook was ready, too. He intended to make maps such as he had made before, and whenever he found himself underneath the same portion of the map again, he would mark the point with an X and flip to the next page. Nelson was relying on his chalk, as before.

They parked their car in the usual place, climbed the hill to the entrance, and almost by instinct took a long look around them at the outside world. Then they went inside, and within a few minutes were down at the junction where Ted wanted to turn right. He had his notebook out, and was beginning a new map.

The right-hand corridor offered nothing unusual, except that it was remarkably long and took a number of turns, all of which Ted carefully noted. There was nothing for Nelson to do for a while, for there were no branches leading off it. They were going downhill at a fairly steep rate. It would have taken strong, sure-footed mules to haul coal up this incline, if that had once been done. It must have been a long time ago, for the tracks had been taken up and no trace of them remained.

Then they reached a room, and could tell that this had once been the scene of major diggings. Walls of black, with doors through some of them, still remained, and they seemed to be walking on pure coal.

"Too bad they had to leave all this coal behind them," Nelson commented. "I suppose safety required it, but strip mining would have got it all."

"Maybe strip-mining machinery came along too late, and the mine was too exhausted by then to make it pay. And I imagine there are limits to how deep you would care to go with strip mining."

"I wonder how many levels there are below this one? Are we down to the bottom of the hill yet, Ted?"

"I don't think so, but we're pretty deep. You're probably right about other levels. Notice how level *this* floor is. I suppose it was done that way on purpose, so there'd be no difficulty calculating the distance between the floor here and the ceiling below."

"And I hope somebody calculated it just right. This time I'm on the side of mathematics."

One room led directly on to another, and each room had numerous doors. They supposed it was handy to have several routes for taking out the coal, as well as a safety precaution. They couldn't tell whether there was any way to get outside other than by the long path they had come. There was no sign of such an entrance.

"Holy smokes, Ted! I nearly made a bad mistake. Where there are several doors, I have to mark not only the door we go out of, but the one that brought us in. If I didn't, we might return to this room, and wouldn't know which one to take."

"We've got my maps, Nel."

"Sure, but I like to be doubly safe. It's a good thing I thought of that. I hope I haven't slipped up."

They passed through six, seven, eight rooms, before Ted suddenly called a halt. "Do you know where we are, Nel?"

"No, should I?"

"This is the same room we were in about fifteen minutes ago, according to my map. We've come right around in a circle."

Nelson found some of his own marks on one of the doors on the opposite side of the room. They were glad to see that Ted's maps had proved accurate.

"Should we try one of these other doors, Ted?"

"I'm afraid it all seems to be pretty much of the same thing. Just one room after another, all interconnected. Let's go back a way, and see if we can't find something different."

They did, and taking a little side room they had bypassed before, they found a door opposite that led into another long, descending tunnel. There were no side paths, and by the time they reached the bottom, they knew they had found a new level. They felt a little cooler and damper than they had before, and wondered if perhaps they were reaching the level of the river itself.

"Wouldn't water seep in if we did, Nel?"

"Not necessarily. We build tunnels beneath rivers, and they don't leak. I imagine nature could do the same thing. The rock might be water-tight, at least in certain layers. But maybe there is some seepage, for Mr. Winslow mentioned pumps."

This level seemed to be almost a duplicate of the one above, as though it had been planned by the same engineer. They investigated a few of the rooms—all of them apparently mined out many years ago—without discovering anything new enough to interest them. They still had found no way to reach the outside world, other than the long, roundabout route they had come.

Understanding the layout of the mine a little better now, they had no trouble finding another corridor that led them down to a still lower level.

"Holy Moses, Ted, how many more of these levels are there?"

"I don't know, but let's make this the last one for us. After we've looked around here, we'll go back up."

The tunnel led into a few rooms that had been mined out and seemed to lead nowhere. These rooms were less extensive than the ones above. Another corridor led away from them, level this time rather than descending, and seemed to lead to another section of the mine.

"Let's follow this for a while, Nel, but if we find it going down, we quit and go back."

"You bet," Nelson agreed emphatically. "We must have covered about three miles altogether, and it's probably nearly a mile back to the surface, even by the most direct route we know of. No wonder the miners want portal-to-portal pay, when they have to go so far to their work."

Some distance down the corridor they encountered something that surprised them. There was a large wooden door that, when closed, would have blocked the tunnel efficiently and completely. Was it a fire door? If so, surely it would have been made out of something more resistant than wood. A sign painted on it in large warning letters read:

DANGER

THIS DOOR MUST BE KEPT CLOSED ALWAYS

And yet the door was standing wide open.

"What do you make of that, Ted? Should we close the door? At least I'm glad to see there isn't any lock on it. That means it isn't intended to block off anyone's retreat."

"That's probably exactly why they don't have a lock on it. I have an idea what it is, though. It's an air door. The door is kept closed so that when the air-conditioning equipment is turned on, the airflow won't find a short circuit this way, when it's intended to flush out a more roundabout section. I suppose there are many of these doors down below, where the mine was worked more recently. By opening and closing them in different combinations, they can air out any portion of the mine that they want to."

"Do we close it, then?"

"No, it was probably opened by a maintenance man, and he must know what he is doing. After all, if a door was really meant never to be opened, there wouldn't be any point in having a door."

They went on through the open doorway, the corridor continuing to twist about. They passed some side tunnels, but decided to ignore these. They were looking for more signs of coal mining, trying to reach the section where the big mining had been going on before the closing.

Presently the corridor divided into two lanes. Which way to go, or should they go at all? They were pretty tired, and it was getting on toward evening, if that meant anything in a coal mine.

"We'll make this the last one, positively," Ted decided, and Nelson agreed. "As soon as we come to a room, or another branch, that's it. This map is beginning to look like a maze, and I don't want to complicate it too much."

Which one to try? Ted suggested the left one, while Nelson suggested the right at almost the same instant. They were too tired to disagree with each other. Ted, who was standing on the left, turned to the right, at precisely the same moment that Nelson turned to the left. They collided, and both dropped their flashlights, which were immediately extinguished.

Complete silence reigned in the darkness for a few moments. Then each one started to speak at the same moment, not quite willing to admit the desperation of their predicament:

"What . . . what happened?"

CHAPTER 13.

THE SOUND OF HEAVENLY MUSIC

THEY quickly realized they must size up their situation carefully and rationally. This was hard to do, for they had never experienced such intense darkness before. Their eyes rebelled at it, and for a few minutes lights flashed just as though the tunnel were full of flickering beams, dancing about at random, elusive, teasing to be caught. Then this stopped.

"Don't move, Ted, not even a step," Nelson warned him. "The first thing to do is to retrieve our flashlights. Maybe all that happened is that the bulbs are broken, and we can replace them."

But they both heard the flashlights hit the hard ground with a solid crash, and knew that it didn't take much of a jolt to disconnect the circuit on a flashlight. They stooped down and began to feel along the ground. Ted soon recovered one of them, but the other had rolled a few feet away. Nelson had to feel a short distance in several directions before he finally regained it.

"Ouch!" he exclaimed. "Cut myself."

"Very badly?"

"I don't know. Turn on the lights and I'll see." But his cut was evidently nothing to worry about, in view of their far greater troubles. "Now, Ted, let's sit down on the ground facing each other, with our legs touching, and we'll put all the parts between our legs so we can't lose them. Just hold on to your flashlight for a minute, and I'll see what I can do with mine. The glass is broken, of course, but I'm screwing off the top so I can change bulbs without cutting myself. All right. Now I'll take out the old bulb. It's broken, too."

"Don't cut yourself."

"I'm using a handkerchief on it. It's hard, but now it's coming. There. I've got a fresh bulb out of my pocket now, and I'm screwing it in. No, it still doesn't light." He tried not to sound disappointed. "All right, Ted, we'll try the same thing with your flashlight. Want me to do it?"

"No, I'll try it myself." Ted repeated the same operation, with the same result. "Mine isn't going to work either. What more can we do about it, Nel? Is there any way to fix the flashlights?"

"I don't know yet. Sometimes if you just bang them around a little, you can get them going again. We'll have plenty of time to try that later, if nothing else works. Do you think putting in fresh batteries might help any, Ted?"

"I never knew that batteries could get broken from a short drop like that, but let's try it anyway." They did, but with no success.

"All right, then, Ted, we'll have to see what else we can think of. We don't have any matches, or any way of starting a fire—which may be just as well. What do we have? We've got plenty of batteries and bulbs. Actually, you don't even need a flashlight case. You just put a bulb on top of a battery or two, and then you connect the bulb to the bottom of a battery with a little piece of wire, and you're in business. What have you got in your pockets, Ted? You must have a paper clip. You always carry paper clips with you."

"No, when I took these clothes to the laundry I cleaned out the pockets. I don't have a clip."

"You're sure about that, Ted? This might be awfully important."

"No, no clip—but I'll never be without one again."

"All right, no clip. Now tell me everything you do have."

"I've got my notebook—"

"Metal rings?"

"No, this is my stitched one. And I have two pencils."

"Metal?"

"No, one is a wooden pencil, and the other one is made out of plastic. Not even a metal clip on it."

"But there might be a metal spiral inside."

"I don't know about that. If there is, we might have a devil of a time getting it out."

"Go on. What other metal have you got?"

"My wallet, with a metal snap on it. A belt buckle. How about the zipper on my jacket?"

"That won't do. There are gaps between the teeth. What else?"

"Some pocket change. Silver is a good conductor of electricity, if we could only assemble a string on a piece of tape, but we can't. There's my wristwatch, but the band is leather, the tips of my shoe laces, and maybe a couple of silver fillings in my teeth, and that's all the metal I've got on me."

"Let's see if I can do any better. I've got just about the same inventory, plus the chalk and extra batteries and bulbs I'm carrying. If worse comes to worst, we might be able to smash up one of the flashlight cases, in the hope of getting out a piece of metal that we could use. But we won't do that unless we're completely desperate. It's too much like burning your bridges behind you. Right now let's try banging the flashlights on the ground a little. How do you rate our chances of getting found, Ted?"

"Well, this mine isn't exactly uninhabited. There are maintenance men around, there are the pirates, there is a ghost, in case he comes back. But it's an awfully big place, too. We might be in an abandoned part of it that doesn't get visited every week, or even every month. There's no telling how long it would be before someone stumbled across us. But what about someone coming in search of us, Nel?"

"Our car might be sitting out there anywhere from three days to a week before someone reports it to the police or they spot it themselves. Then they're likely to tow it in, and might or might not notify our families while they waited for us to turn up. It could be another week before anything was done."

"Wouldn't they connect an abandoned car with the mine, long before that?"

"I don't know how long you mean, Ted. Especially with the coal pirates around, they might not be particularly anxious to see too much. The point is, we don't know how long it'll be, but we can't count on having that much time. Who else besides the police? The motel keeper? I don't think he would give us a thought, as long as our rent's paid up in advance. When that time is up, he might be satisfied to hold our luggage for a while, and my camera's worth good money. What about Mr. Dobson?"

"He doesn't expect to hear from me every day. If he thought I was particularly busy winding up on a story, it might be a week before he began to worry seriously about us. Probably the same thing goes with our families. They know we're working, and that satisfies them."

"I don't think I'm going to be able to coax this flashlight back into operation, but let's trade, just for luck. Who else might find us?"

"At least we've got those marks on the walls you made working for us. Just in case someone *did* come looking for us, there shouldn't be too much of a problem about it."

"I hope you're right, Ted, but I've got a sneaking suspicion that maybe I made a mistake someplace. It wouldn't be too important to us, because we had your map and our memories to help us. But it would only take a small error to throw the whole thing off for someone looking for us."

"I guess it adds up to the fact that there's a chance someone might find us, but we can't count on it. So we'd better consider our chances for finding our own way out. That offers two possibilities: to go forward, or to go backward."

"Which looks better to you, Ted?"

"Going back has certain advantages. We've been there before, and have at least an idea about things. And we're staying within the area where we've made our markings, so that we'd have a better chance of being found by someone looking for us. But when I remember all the places to make a wrong turn, and know that only one mistake would be too many, I just can't see how we'll make it.

"Going ahead looks attractive because for all we know there might be an entrance to the mine just a short way ahead of us. Or we might get into a part of the mine where someone was working. Even coal pirates would look pretty good to me now!

"But I suppose our chances of finding another entrance are really pretty small. We're down deep here. I don't know whether we're below the level of the river or not, but at least we know we have a big hill sitting on top of us. There might be open pits or stale or contaminated air ahead of us. And I'm not sure we could mark our trail so that anyone following us could stay with us. That's how I size it up. What would be your vote?"

"The same as yours, Ted. If we try to find our own way out, I guess it would be better to go back. Then the question is, how long do we wait here before we make our move?"

"It can't be too long. It's a long way back to the surface, and we have to make it while we still have enough energy and before we get knocked out by thirst. That gives us maybe three days to do it in, and we may need every minute of it. How long do you think we should fool with the flashlights, Nel?"

"Let's see, at least we can tell time with these illuminated dials. Suppose you give me two hours to see if I can rig up something. If I can't do it by then, we'll give it up and start hunting for our way back. I suppose we could walk along side by side, with you feeling along one wall while I felt along the other. We could take note of every turnoff, and reach a decision about it. But distances are awfully deceptive in the dark."

Nelson set to work with the flashlights, but just what he was trying to do Ted did not know. Except to hand Nelson something that he asked for from time to time, Ted took no part in the operation, trusting more in Nelson's mechanical abilities than in his own. All he was sure of was that Nelson had not yet pounded one of the flashlights apart.

Occasionally they heard a noise—probably, they decided, the groaning or creaking of the supports as the temperature changed, and a few times they heard pebbles fall. This could be a natural thing, or there might be rats or other small animals scurrying about in the darkness.

"Listen!" said Ted suddenly.

Nelson did, for at least half a minute. "I don't hear anything."

"No, I don't either now. Wait . . . there it goes again. Hear it?"

"Yes. What is it? It sounds a little bit like music. What could it be?"

"Heavenly music, the sweetest music ever heard," said Ted, his voice more optimistic than it had been since the lights went out. "That's a bell . . . a tinkling bell . . . it sounds like Alice's bell!"

"Alice! Say, Ted, I believe you're right. Is she coming this way?"

"I—I *think* so. Listen, Nel, grab up everything and stick it in your pockets. We may need it later. Got everything?"

"Yes, I guess so. She's still coming, isn't she?"

"Yes, but in her own good time."

The boys stood up. They found that it was not easy to keep their balance in the dark, and even small obstacles, as they took a few steps, threw them off stride.

"How'll we handle Alice, Ted? We've got to be careful not to spook her off. But she knows us already, so that might not be too bad."

"Don't touch her, whatever you do, Nel."

"Why's that, Ted?"

"Because the minute you touch her she'll think you're trying to guide her, and it becomes a case of the blind leading the blind. We've got to be careful that she goes exactly where *she* wants to go."

"She must be almost here. Let's keep talking, Ted, so our voices don't suddenly startle her."

They did so, and though Alice must have heard them now, it did not seem to frighten her or cause her to change either her pace or her course. She was very close now. They thought they could even hear her breathing. They pulled back against the wall, so that Alice would pass them, and then they could follow her. To their great surprise, Alice did not pass them, but turned the Y and headed down the other corridor.

"She's taking us into the strange part of the mine. Quick, Nel, we've only got a few seconds to decide, and it may be a matter of life or death. Do we follow Alice blindly, or do we wait around for some human beings to find us?"

"Right now I'd rather trust Alice than people. But don't let me have the whole say."

"We follow Alice then!"

They did not want to follow so closely as to alarm the mule, nor did they want to lose her. They hurried after her until they were some twenty feet behind her, and then they slowed their pace to match hers, talking quietly the while.

"You know that air door, Nel? It's usually closed, and maybe Alice knows it. She has to go a different way."

"I only hope she knows what she's doing. Do you think she can see any better in the dark than we can, Ted?"

"No, not when it's as black as this. But her hearing may be a good deal better. Blind people often do well by listening for echoes. And it may be that she has this whole course memorized. She worked down here for many years."

They found it best to drag their feet along as they walked, thus kicking aside small stones or feeling their way cautiously over larger ones. A sprained ankle wasn't a pleasant thought, and a straggler would have to be left behind while the other one went for help. Alice seemed much more sure of foot than they, and never faltered. Making turns offered a ticklish problem in the dark, and occasionally her bell stopped tinkling, giving them a momentary scare, but it soon commenced again as she regained her former stride. She seemed to have no fear of these people she must know by now were following her. Whatever was going on in her mulish mind, she was intent upon it. They hoped that she was heading home for supper.

They were lost through the myriad of turnings, but they had a feeling of climbing, which was a good sign. Had they come a half mile . . . a mile? It was hard to guess in the dark. About half an hour had passed since they had chosen Alice as their guide, but it was hard to translate time into distance.

And then they made a turn, and there was daylight ahead! Furthermore, they found, as they neared the opening, that it was the same entrance they had used.

"I guess we did it," said Nelson in an awed voice.

"Yes, we did. I've got a feeling, though, that Alice brought us back through the left turn, not through the right turn where we went down."

"Whatever it was, she did just right. If I ever want to give my grandchildren any advice, I'll tell them this: 'When you get in trouble, always trust a mule.'"

CHAPTER 14.

THE MILLION-DOLLAR SECRET

ALICE, as it turned out, was wearing a halter, and they led her down the hill to the car. She seemed satisfied to go in this direction, so they had no trouble; had she been determined to go elsewhere there might have been difficulties.

"I don't think Alice is obstinate, Ted," Nelson observed. "She's just stubborn."

"Is there a difference?"

"Sure. A stubborn person wants his own way; an obstinate person wants the opposite of whatever other people want. We're not going to turn Alice loose to find her own way home, are we? We owe her more than that."

"You bet we do," said Ted. "Traffic might be harder for her to cope with than all the dangers of a coal mine. Why don't I lead her home, while you go along in the car? If we both walk, we'll have to come back for the car."

"Nothing doing, Ted. I've fallen in love with Alice. You drive and I'll walk. There's something for us to decide first, though. How much of this are we going to tell anybody?"

"Let's not tell. It would only alarm our folks and Mr. Dobson. I'd like to give credit where credit is due, but I don't think Alice will mind a bit. We can just say we found her while she was on her way out of the mine. After all, all that really happened is that we're getting back an hour later than we planned. But after we're home and cleaned up, we're going to have to do some pretty clear thinking. I still want to know what Alice was doing in that mine."

Ted drove on ahead to tell the Llewellyns their mule had been found and was being returned to them. Joyce and Johnny had been sad over the latest disappearance of their mule, but had been barred by the strictest of promises to their mother from setting out in search of her. Now their sober faces lit up with happy smiles when Ted told them the news.

Although Mrs. Llewellyn invited the boys to stay for supper, they declined with thanks. They felt very dirty, and Ted wanted to call Forestdale before Sergeant Jeffers went off duty. He made the call from a booth on the way home.

"I think I've got what you want, Ted," the sergeant said. "The man's name is Professor Walberg Thomas. He's a professor of geology and paleontology up at Usher. As far as I know, he's a perfectly responsible man, and has never had any trouble with the police. Is that what you wanted to know?"

"Yes, that's exactly what I wanted. Thanks a lot, Sergeant Jeffers."

But Ted's voice was dull as he relayed this report to Nelson. "So you see, there was nothing in our ghost after all. He's just a professor interested in fossils, and of course coal itself is a form of fossil."

"So we cross Professor Thomas off our list?"

"You mean the list for my newspaper story? Might as well. I don't see how he is going to be of any use to us. I'm much more interested in Alice right now."

"What about Alice, Ted?"

But Ted refused to say anything more until they had cleaned up, gone out for dinner, and returned to the cabin. He wanted to get the thing a little clearer in his own mind.

"I wonder if we didn't begin our whole chain of reasoning on a false premise," Ted began. "Our first idea was that when Joyce and Johnny ran into the mine after their mule, they had made a mistake. How do we know they made a mistake? It's possible they were right and we were wrong. It was nearly pitch black in that tunnel, and I just don't believe they would have had the courage to go on, unless they were pretty positive that Alice was in the mine. And we finally got our proof today that Alice *did* visit the mine once in a while at least. So let's say that Alice was in the mine, and spent the night there, which is the reason she didn't get wet in the storm."

"Go on, Ted," said Nelson, all attention.

"Well, what was on Alice's mind? She was attracted by that fresh green grass across the river, and wasn't going to let anything swerve her. And our proof there is that she did reach the nice grass, and was found there the next morning. So we have our mine on one side of the river, and the grass on the other side. The problem is to connect the two."

"How do you connect them, Ted?"

"Why, I'd connect them with a tunnel under the river."

"Hey! Ted!" Nelson pounded his leg with his fist. "Now how about that?"

"If that's the truth of the matter, we've solved our little puzzle. But this raises another question: does this matter? Is it of any importance?"

"Is it, Ted?" Nelson returned, undecided.

"Who knew about the tunnel, and what was he doing about it? It doesn't seem to be general knowledge. Mrs. Llewellyn didn't know about it, and neither did Mr. Stevens. In fact, we've talked to quite a few people, and no one has ever mentioned it to us. But who ought to know about the tunnel? It must come up somewhere in West Walton, on Mr. Sorrel's property. He's been all over that property so many times, surely he ought to know about it if anybody does, but apparently he isn't saying a thing."

"Why not, Ted?"

"Why don't we ask him?"

Nelson was enthusiastic, and Ted put through the call, asking if he might interview Mr. Sorrel that evening. At first Mr. Sorrel wanted to know why Ted couldn't ask him whatever it was over the phone. But Ted explained that it was rather complicated, and managed to rouse his curiosity enough so that he consented to the interview.

At Mr. Sorrel's home they were invited to sit down, but he said he would appreciate it if they would come directly to the point.

"I'll do just that, Mr. Sorrel," said Ted. "The fact is that we know about the tunnel under the river."

Mr. Sorrel looked from one to the other and then seemed to deflate like a flat tire.

"So you know about the tunnel. I don't know how much else you know, but that doesn't matter because you can easily get the rest of it now. I may as well tell you the whole truth. It isn't just a tunnel. It's an old coal mine, a whole network of tunnels running beneath my property. The mine wasn't as profitable as the one on this side of the river, and was abandoned over fifty years ago.

"I don't think anyone around here remembers that there was once some mining on the other side of the river. But the tunnels are still there. I knew nothing about that when I bought and leased and optioned the property, scraping up every cent I could beg, borrow, or connive." He laughed bitterly. "So everybody thinks *I* cheated the people I bought from. Look what they did to me."

"Are you sure they knew about the tunnels?" Ted questioned.

"Of course they did!"

"Is the situation really bad?"

"Bad? Just picture it: you show a prospect a forty-thousand-dollar home. He says it's just what he wanted, and asks if anything is wrong with it. So you tell him, 'Oh, there's one small thing. There is an old coal mine running under the property.' If you can catch his coat tails before he starts running, the first thing you do is to knock ten thousand dollars off the purchase price. Then, maybe, he'll show a small spark of interest again. I was planning on putting up a hundred homes. Multiply ten thousand dollars by a hundred, and what do you get?"

"A million dollars," said Ted, while Nelson was still trying to calculate the correct number of zeroes.

"That's right. My secret was worth a million dollars to me. You wonder that I tried to hang on to it?"

"Wasn't it a dangerous thing to do?"

"Dangerous for those who might buy the property? Of course not. There's no danger from the mine. The tunnels are all deep, the rocks are solid, the coal was never over-mined. That ground is just as safe as any other ground you might care to mention."

"Why is it that no one on this side of the river knew about the tunnel?"

"Because the tunnel wasn't there. Remember that big explosion? That was what knocked out the wall between the two old mines and joined them. In exploring the abandoned mine a week or so before the explosion, I discovered a pocket of gas. That was the reason for my inquiries about gas and explosions. Then, before anything could be done, the explosion came, apparently touched off by mining operations coming through from the other side. Of course I had no idea at all that the mining was that close to my property. If you wonder why I was so bitter over people accusing me, it was because I knew I *was* guilty. I was the only one who could have prevented the accident."

"Didn't you ever try to explain?"

"Would people have believed me if I did? And I couldn't say anything without giving away my secret. I thought surely someone would soon discover it, but it seemed that no one did. There were safety inspections, of course, but the inspectors all went in from this side. It was assumed that the mine had happened to connect up with an old abandoned section, but no one explored it thoroughly to see just where this other section went. The miners never went down again after the explosion, of course; even the coal pirates operate a considerable distance away."

He hesitated. "I said I'd tell you the whole story, Ted, and I will. There's one person who knows—because he's been blackmailing me."

"Blackmail! Who is the person?"

"That I don't know. I send twenty-five dollars a week in a blank envelope to a post office box in some other city. You can't very easily find out the name of a box-holder, and though I made an attempt to watch the box for a while, the blackmailer didn't make a practice of picking up his mail regularly or promptly, so I never caught him. He's not being terribly exorbitant—for now. But he's told me frankly that he's not going to be satisfied with this sum. He wants me to deed one of my houses over to him, and that will end the matter. It probably would, too, because after that, once I closed my deals, it probably wouldn't matter."

"Did you agree to his terms?"

"I've been making the weekly payments," Mr. Sorrel said slowly. "I haven't made any commitment about the house yet. A forty-thousand-dollar loss to protect a million-dollar profit might be a good bargain, if everything turned out right. But I don't like it. I thought that if I could find out who the blackmailer is, I could threaten to expose *him,* and that might shut him up."

Ted stood up and so did the others.

"Do you intend to print the story?" asked Mr. Sorrel. "I mean about the tunnels, of course. If that part of the story comes out, the blackmailer won't be able to hurt me any more."

"I couldn't say, Mr. Sorrel. That decision will be up to Mr. Dobson."

Then they all said good night on a fairly cordial note.

"That's a pretty big secret," Nelson offered. "I don't see how he could ever hope to keep it, do you? But of all the people who might have told that secret, Ted—Mr. Sorrel, or the farmers, or the blackmailer, or almost anybody who happened to stumble across that tunnel in the mine—none of them did. It was Alice who let the secret out of the bag."

CHAPTER 15.

DIRTY HANDS

NEXT morning they realized they would have to think about getting home. Ted had pounded out a good many rough pages of his story and his notebook was crammed with notes. Nelson had taken more pictures than Mr. Dobson would be able to use. They had picked up the atmosphere of East Walton and the coal mine, were acquainted with its problems, and had heard several possible solutions.

"You do have a story, don't you, Ted—a really good one?"

"Well, I think I have a few things that will surprise people, if that's what you mean. There's the part about the coal pirates, and about the tunnels under Mr. Sorrel's property, if Mr. Dobson decides to use it. Alice would make a good feature story all by herself. I guess my big disappointment is about something I didn't have any right to expect anyway: I don't have any real answer to the problems of East Walton."

"So what, Ted? Neither does anyone else, and you're not Houdini. What do we still need?"

"Just a few more interviews, and then I guess we've had it. Maybe we can wind up today, and leave tomorrow."

"Will we be leaving any unfinished business behind us, Ted?"

"Some, I suppose, but I don't see how it can be helped. I'd like to know who was blackmailing Mr. Sorrel. But it's been going on a long time, and he couldn't find out, so how can we?"

"Are you sure we can trust Mr. Sorrel?" asked Nelson. "Wasn't he really trying to cheat people?"

Ted rubbed his head. "I don't know anything about the legal end of it. The important thing, I guess, is that he hasn't cheated anybody yet, and we can't be sure he ever will. He probably doesn't even know for sure himself. I think he was telling us the truth, though.

There wouldn't be any reason to lie about the blackmailer, once we had found out about the tunnels."

"Do you suppose the blackmailer is somebody in East Walton?"

"By all odds it ought to be," said Ted. "The secret is here, so why not the blackmailer? The fact that he doesn't go to his postal box very often may mean that he has trouble getting there."

"Isn't there any way Mr. Sorrel could catch him?"

"I doubt it, not by himself. The blackmailer is probably pretty well acquainted with Mr. Sorrel's movements, and wouldn't go to the box unless he was quite certain Mr. Sorrel was busy elsewhere. The name of the box-holder is probably a phony, so all you could hope to do is catch him in the act."

"But the name would come out when he signed over the property, wouldn't it?"

"Maybe not even then. He might have some friend to stand in for him as front man."

"I think there's one more piece of unfinished business, Ted. Who was trying to run us out of town? Are you certain it wasn't Mr. Sorrel? He was the one who had the big secret we were threatening to uncover."

"There's a chance that it was, I suppose, though I hate to think so. Mr. Sorrel seemed to talk pretty frankly with us last night."

"Because he knew you had him in a corner anyway, Ted," Nelson quickly pointed out. "Maybe he realized it was too late, or he may have other secrets that he isn't talking about."

"Yes, and so might anyone else in town."

Looking at his hands, Ted noticed coal dust deeply imbedded in the knuckles. It was the sort of thing that didn't come out with just one washing, no matter how vigorous. Nelson's hands were even worse, having been compounded with oil as he did a little tinkering with his car. Though Ted wanted to appear as presentable as possible at his interviews, Nelson didn't think it mattered.

"People are used to that, especially in a mining town. Mr. Allen told us they're even suspicious about a person whose hands are too clean."

The interviews went off quite well. Ted was able to ask questions with more assurance, because he knew what he was talking about, and had a better idea what he was trying to find out. They completed their interviews about the middle of the afternoon, then stopped at the drugstore. Phil was on duty, and served them sundaes, with some fancy extras, on the house. They discussed with him their work up to date, although they didn't tell him anything about the secrets they had discovered.

"Has Mr. Winslow put that barricade back up at the mine yet, Ted?"

"Not as far as I know."

"I wish he would. I don't like the idea of small children wandering in there. I think he'd do it pronto, if you threatened to put an item in the paper."

Was Phil making too much of a small thing?

"Why don't you do it, Phil? You're the local correspondent. And if he doesn't put it back, send in the item, and we may use it. That way it won't be just an idle threat."

"All right, Ted, I'll do that. You made me forget for a while that I was a reporter here, too. I take it you're about ready to leave, then?"

"Very soon. But we'll be in touch with you before we go."

Back at their cabin they threw themselves on their beds for a short rest. Nelson made several remarks, but Ted was so unresponsive, he asked:

"What's the matter with you, Ted? Too much ice cream?"

"I want to talk about Phil," Ted answered, looking unhappy. "Did you notice that when he dished up our ice cream his hands were dirty?"

"Is that all?" Nelson was about to explode into laughter, then quickly subsided as he realized there was more to it than that. "What are you getting at?"

"Phil had that same kind of dust in his knuckles that we have even after a good scrubbing. I think he was down in the mine this morning."

"Go on, Ted."

"Let's review everything that has happened to us in East Walton, and try to see it in a different light. At first we thought that perhaps Phil would be bitter about my coming into his territory, but he wasn't. He couldn't have been friendlier or more cooperative."

"No harm in that, is there?"

"In Phil's place I might have been annoyed at another reporter's coming into my territory, but he didn't seem to mind. Maybe it was because he had to give all his attention to hiding something big from us.

"First the gun was planted on us. Phil certainly had the opportunity. He was at the Canteen with us, and left before we did. He could easily have gone out to the parking lot and put the gun inside your car. You admit your door wouldn't be hard to force."

"He had the opportunity, Ted, but did he have the gun?"

"He said the gun was taken from his store in a burglary, but how do we know that it was ever stolen, that there even was a burglary?"

"This was before he knew we were coming to East Walton, Ted. He couldn't have known then that he would want to plant a gun on us."

"I wonder if maybe he did know, stumbled across our car parked near the mine or something like that. It's true that he came down to the station and apparently did his best to clear us. What else could he do? But how do we know he wasn't the person who called the station anonymously? Assuming that the plot took a little advance preparation, who else knew ahead of time that we would be at the Canteen?"

"It could have been done by someone who didn't know, but was out looking for an opportunity, Ted."

"Yes, I know. All right, here's my next point: the phone call I got about Doctor Clifford. I wonder if Phil didn't push his luck a little too far on that? We assumed that it was someone else trying to make his voice sound like Phil's, but how do we know it wasn't Phil, trying to disguise his voice? If it was anyone beside Phil, he was taking a big chance. How could he know I hadn't just talked with Phil? How could he know that I wouldn't refer back to something that had been said between us that would expose him? All right, let's just say he took a chance because he didn't have anything to lose—I probably couldn't catch him anyway. He would have to know so much about what had happened between Phil and me, and how our newspaper worked, about my intention to call the *Town Crier*—it's just incredible that anyone else could have done it. This idea has been nagging at the back of my mind, long before I noticed Phil's dirty knuckles.

"My next point has to do with my notebook. He left the tennis game and went back to the drugstore. But we returned before he expected us, and my notebook wasn't in my pocket. I didn't miss it at once, and he called to say I dropped it. But isn't it more likely that he took it out himself?"

"Why, Ted?"

"The maps, I suppose. He wanted to see if we had gone, or were likely to go, anywhere near the secret tunnel. But we went back into the mine again yesterday, and this time he didn't have much hope of getting my notebook again. Still there were the chalk marks you had made on the wall. We had told him how we were doing it, and he could follow those marks to see how far we had gone."

"I wonder if he knew that we were trapped there in the dark, Ted?"

"I don't think he would have found it out today. When the marks ran out, he would assume that was as far as we had traveled, and then turned around and gone back."

"You believe he knows about the tunnel, Ted?"

"He must have. As a reporter for the old East Walton paper, he helped investigate the explosion, so he had an excellent chance to find out. And of course if he's the blackmailer—" Nelson sat bolt upright. "Yes, I was leading up to the blackmail, of course. If he was the blackmailer, then it was his secret, too, as much as Mr. Sorrel's, and he wouldn't want us to find out. That was the reason he was anxious to get us out of town as soon as he could. I think he gave us the item about Doctor Clifford to help make Mr. Dobson impatient with us so he would call us home.

"And my final point. He showed special interest in getting that barricade back up again. He probably didn't want Alice taking that short cut over to the other side of the river, and giving away the whole show.

"That's my case, Nel. How does it sound to you?"

Nelson considered for several minutes. "You've got a good many points, Ted," he admitted finally. "The trouble is you don't have any real proof, nothing that you could accuse Phil of, nothing that you could take into court."

"I know," Ted agreed, "but I think I know how we can get some proof. Want to try it?"

Nelson agreed with a wave of his hand, and Ted went to the telephone to dial the drugstore's number.

"Phil, this is Ted. We're leaving a little sooner than we planned, so I wanted to say goodbye and thank you for everything you did for us. Nelson says to thank you especially for the ice cream, so you know where his mind is."

"Oh, I didn't do very much, Ted. I'm sorry you're going, but look me up again whenever you're in the neighborhood."

"I'll do that, Phil, and you do the same in Forestdale. . . . Oh, a funny little thing just happened. The Llewellyns called to tell me their mule got out again, and wanted to know if I'd seen her. They must think I'm in the mule-finding business. I'm afraid I won't have any time to bother with that now. Anyway, Alice always seems to find her own way home."

They said goodbye, and hung up.

Nelson had been hanging close to Ted's elbow. "What do we do now?" he demanded.

"We race out to the mine. If Phil is really interested in keeping Alice out of the mine, he'll be rushing out there to head her off."

They got out to the mine as fast as the speed laws would allow, drove a little past it and pulled off the road to a spot where Phil could not see the car but from which they could see him. They did not have long to wait. Phil's car soon came roaring up. He, too, pulled off the road where his car was reasonably concealed, then hurried up the hill toward the mine entrance.

"I guess that clinches your case," said Nelson. "What's the next step?"

"I like to handle my own stories, but it's only smart to know when you need help. I'm going to put in a call to Mr. Dobson."

CHAPTER 16.

TIME TO BAKE THE PIE

TED put through his call to Mr. Dobson and explained matters briefly. It seemed to the editor that it would be best for him to come up to East Walton at once. As Ted relayed this information to Nelson, he felt he had taken on a good deal of responsibility. Never before had he run to his editor for help in quite this manner, but they were facing a grave situation.

Since it would be several hours before Mr. Dobson would arrive, they had supper, and then Ted went to work at his story in a desultory fashion, while Nelson puttered with his pictures and other odds and ends.

When a knock came on the door, they knew it was too soon for Mr. Dobson. Rising to answer, Ted hoped fervently that it wouldn't be Phil, for he didn't yet know what to do about him.

But it was Professor Thomas.

"I'm not going to give you my name, because I'm sure you know it already. I've got that much respect for your detective ability."

"And I might add the same about you," Ted conceded.

"Yes, I was wondering who those two persons were who frightened me away from my lunch in the mine. I wasn't sure, until I noticed your unusual interest in me in the park. Just what attracted you?"

"The orange lunch box," Nelson explained.

Professor Thomas laughed. "So that was it. I hadn't thought you came far enough into the room to discover it. At any rate I decided it would be just as well to let you get my license number, while I waited outside the parking lot to get yours."

Then the three of them laughed together as the professor fitted names to faces.

"Ted," he began, "I might say that though I've never met your Mr. Dobson, I've heard a good deal about him, and have the highest respect for him. Now let me ask you a question: what do you know about the coal pirates?"

"I understand there is a continuous operation going on down there," said Ted.

"There's the cautious journalist. Continuous, of course, but on how large a scale? Do you know how they are hauling their coal away?"

Ted studied the professor and could see that he already knew about the barge.

"I believe they do it on the river."

"Of course, of course." Professor Thomas nodded his approval. "I see I didn't make a mistake in coming here. Now why is it that Mr. Winslow isn't worried about the pirate operation?"

"Because he doesn't know about the barge?"

"Right, Ted. Any other reason?"

"Not that I know of," said Ted in surprise.

"Well, it's a relief to me that I do know something you don't know. The truth is, Ted, that even if Mr. Winslow knew about the barge I don't think he would be greatly concerned. He would still figure it couldn't be a big enough operation to worry about. But he would be wrong. There's a big secret down there that he doesn't know about.

"I'm sure that the pirates began on a small scale and in a quite random fashion, digging a little here and a little there, without getting away with much. But that isn't what they are doing now. The digging is all centralized at a certain location. The pirates discovered a rich new vein of coal of better quality than the mine was producing before, and in a location that offers fewer engineering problems. I'm certain that if Mr. Winslow knew about this fresh lode, he would have reopened the mine years ago. He couldn't afford to keep it shut."

"Well!" Ted was flabbergasted, and Nelson shared his amazement. They had thought that Mr. Sorrel's million-dollar secret was large, but this seemed to be even bigger.

"I'm a geologist and not an engineer, but I'm pretty sure of what I'm talking about." He drew several sheets of paper from his pocket and handed them to Ted. "Here's my preliminary report on the matter. You may keep that copy. The figures and things may not mean much to you, but if you were to take them to a competent engineer, I'm sure he would back me up."

"May I publish your report, Professor Thomas?"

"Certainly, you may, and call it mine. I have some reputation in my field, and I don't think this matter would be dismissed lightly."

"This is extremely kind of you, Professor," said Ted, gratefully. "I'm not used to having scoops like this dropped in my lap."

The professor laughed. "I'm not dropping it in your lap, Ted. You smoked me out. Didn't you discover me in the mine? I suppose the vacationing geology professor puttering around in a coal mine would form an amusing anecdote. However, if you are going to mention me at all, I would prefer to have my work properly appreciated. It was my intention to release my figures a little later, and in a different fashion, but you forced my hand."

Ted still felt overwhelmed by the story the professor had given him. Ted invited him to stay until Mr. Dobson arrived, and he agreed. When the editor arrived, they had an interesting talk. Finally, the professor stood up and announced he had to go. He made his farewells, waving aside the thanks they tried to thrust upon him.

"I'm sure we haven't heard the last of this matter," he said with a grin. "We'll be meeting again."

Then Mr. Dobson and the boys settled down to discuss the situation. After the boys had explained in greater detail just what had occurred, Mr. Dobson had something to add.

"I think I can supply the last link. Phil *did* know you were coming to East Walton. After you left, I decided it would be better for me to call him and smooth things over for you." He paused. "Let's invite both Phil and Mr. Sorrel over here for a conference. I have an idea they'll come."

This prediction was correct, and a little later they all sat down in the cabin, having borrowed extra chairs from the motel manager.

"An editor often faces certain problems," Mr. Dobson began. "I don't expect you to solve my problems for me, but sometimes it helps to consult the persons most directly concerned, just to see how they feel about things.

"I want to tell you about a young man I know. I may even know a little more about him than he realizes. I also know his father. The father was willing to train the boy in the profession that he himself followed, if that was what the boy wanted, even though it meant considerable sacrifice. So the boy went to college, but he didn't stay there long. He has let it be known that he left for lack of money, but this isn't the truth. He flunked out. I have only one explanation for it: that the young man thought he saw a better way to get started without the work and self-sacrifice a professional career would have demanded: in short, by blackmail."

Mr. Sorrel started and gave Phil a sharp look. Phil was sitting without moving, giving no hint of what he was thinking.

"I don't think it necessary just now to go into the nature, method, or victim of this blackmail. I'll pass on instead to a matter that directly concerns my newspaper. Two of my employees were suspected of participation in a robbery because of a gun that was planted on them. It now appears that this gun, previously reported stolen, was in fact never stolen, and that there never was a robbery." He looked at Phil.

"Yes, there was a robbery," Phil insisted. "I made a mistake about the gun, though. It was put away in a different place, so I reported it stolen. Later I found it, but I didn't report I'd found it to the police, as I suppose I should."

"That's a good story, Phil," Mr. Dobson went on. "A few hours ago I wouldn't have dreamed of questioning it. Now I just don't know. At least I ask that you make a report to the police, and admit that you planted the gun on my men. Will you do that, Phil?"

"Yes, sir, I will." Phil's manner was neither disrespectful nor sullen. He was simply reserved. He did not deny the charges, nor admit the blackmail.

"Why did you do it, Phil?" Ted asked him.

"I felt that the story belonged to me," he answered, but no one believed him. The story seemed a small thing; it was exposure about the blackmailing that he feared.

Then Phil got to his feet. "Is that all, sir? Do you have anything else to say?"

"No. I will, of course, check with the police before I leave East Walton, to make sure you do report the matter."

After Phil left, they stared a moment at the closed door.

"What will happen to him now?" Ted speculated.

Mr. Dobson sighed. "He may have learned his lesson and go back to his career. Or he might go from this to something worse. It's really up to him."

He turned to Mr. Sorrel. "You weren't considering a prosecution over the blackmail, were you?"

"How could I? My own hands are none too pure in this business. And it would be difficult to prove in court. I'm willing to forget about what he took from me."

"I'd feel more generous about it if he had wanted the money for his education." Nelson pointed out.

"And now we're faced with your problem, Mr. Sorrel," Mr. Dobson went on. "Have you decided what you're going to do?"

"What can I do? I knew after I talked with Ted last night, something that I probably suspected right along, that I couldn't get away with it. As time went on there was a greater and greater chance that someone would discover that tunnel. I once advised Mr. Winslow to take his losses and go on from there. It might be a good thing for me to take my own advice."

"I'm no lawyer, Mr. Sorrel, so I can't advise you, but I feel that if you did sell property that had a secret and dangerous defect, you might find yourself in trouble."

"But that's the whole point," Mr. Sorrel protested. "There *is* no danger. The explosion cleared up the gas pocket, and even then the surface wasn't disturbed."

"Have you ever had an official inspection of that old mine to make sure of that?"

"Well, no, how could I do that? I was relying on my own knowledge of the situation."

"Then I think you should get some official safety certificates. Maybe it will be necessary to redesign your plans so that no house will be actually built over a tunnel."

Mr. Sorrel acknowledged this argument with a nod.

"There's something else, too," Ted pointed out. "You can prove now that you didn't set off the explosion."

"How can I prove that, Ted?"

"Because you were the last person in the world who would have wanted to open a tunnel between the two mines, and possibly reveal the trouble with your own property."

"You're right, Ted. Maybe it's best to get back in step with the rest of the community."

After Mr. Sorrel had left, Mr. Dobson read through all Ted's notes. They discussed the article—or series of articles—Ted would do, and then he added:

"I think I'm going to break out into a front-page editorial, boys. This mine could have been opened years ago. Mr. Winslow could have opened it, but he was hoping for financial help from the state. The unions wanted it open, but demanded an agreement about job protection from automation first. The coal pirates could have opened it by reporting that new seam, but they were doing well enough with their relief checks and what they made on their pirating, and were afraid if the mine opened they'd lose out to automation. I think Mr. Sorrel would have liked it opened, but he was more concerned with his own projects.

"My point is that the mine stayed closed because there was no one big enough to open it. Everyone was so concerned with dividing up the pie that the pie was never baked. Now it's time to get it in the oven."

Several weeks later Nelson waited outside the building where the legislature was meeting, with more patience than he usually showed. That series of articles in the *Town Crier,* under the by-line of Ted Wilford, had created quite a stir, and a committee had been appointed to investigate the East Walton situation. Professor Thomas had been an earlier witness, and Ted was the next one called.

"How did you make out?" asked Nelson, as Ted finally appeared.

"Pretty well, I guess. They not only wanted to know everything I know, but how I knew it, and what I proposed doing about it."

"What do you think, Ted?"

"Oh, they're a shrewd, hard-hitting bunch, with no nonsense about them. They intend to get to the bottom of this business. I believe they're seriously determined to do something about East Walton, and something will get done. I bet that mine will be open again soon."

"Then I guess we really did something to help the Llewellyn children. If the pie is big enough, they'll get their share."

"And I'm glad to hear that Phil is going back to college," Ted added.